JENNIFER S. ALDERSON

Death by Leprechaun

A Saint Patrick's Day Murder in Dublin

First published by Traveling Life Press 2021

Copyright © 2021 by Jennifer S. Alderson

All rights reserved. No part of this publication may be reproduced, stored or transmitted in any form or by any means, electronic, mechanical, photocopying, recording, scanning, or otherwise without written permission from the publisher. It is illegal to copy this book, post it to a website, or distribute it by any other means without permission.

This novel is entirely a work of fiction. The names, characters and incidents portrayed in it are the work of the author's imagination. Any resemblance to actual persons, living or dead, events or localities is entirely coincidental.

Jennifer S. Alderson asserts the moral right to be identified as the author of this work.

First edition

ISBN: 9798513907220

This book was professionally typeset on Reedsy. Find out more at reedsy.com

Contents

1	To Your Health	1
2	Hair of the Dog	8
3	Holy Namesakes	15
4	Tricksters in Green	22
5	Tap Dancing Seagulls	29
6	Book of Kells	38
7	Miss Me?	45
8	John Doe Investigates	53
9	Breakfast Fit for a King	59
10	Luck of the Irish	63
11	National Leprechaun Museum	66
12	Running Into Guy	69
13	This Is A Crime Scene	77
14	Killers For Clients	87
15	New Evidence	89
16	A Shortage Of Suspects	91
17	A Cathartic Release	96
18	Confidential Sources	100
19	Late for Lunch	109
20	Whiskey and Bacon	111
21	Cooking the Books	116
22	Pinstripe Mafia	120
23	Breaking Up Is Hard To Do	126
24	Music Lessons	133
25	Silver Lining	137
26	Tracing Lineage	141
27	Dubliner	147
28	The Wrong Riley	150

29	Stay or Go	154
30	Family Ties	157
31	Kisses and Wishes in Blarney	163
32	A Parade Fit for a Saint	173
Acknowledgments		177
About the Author		178
Death on the Danube: A New Year's Murder in Budapest		180

1

To Your Health

March 11—Dublin, Ireland

"*Sláinte!*" Wanderlust Tours guide Lana Hansen cried out, mangling the Irish version of "cheers," as she held her pint up high. Three glasses, each as long as her forearm, clinked in the air. Despite the enthusiastic response of her friends, Jeremy and Kitty, Lana could barely hear their hearty replies over the lively Irish music. Everywhere in the pub, patrons were climbing up onto the sturdy wooden chairs and tables to better sing and dance along. In amongst the crowd, Lana could see several members of her tour group clapping and swaying in time with the music, as well.

"I can hardly believe we just flew from the Emerald City to the Emerald Isle," Kitty Tartal yelled over the music before laying her head on her husband's shoulder.

Her words were slightly slurred and her grin goofier than normal. It was understandable; Kitty was working on her second giant pint of cider and was still quite jet-lagged from their flight over from Seattle, Washington.

Lana squeezed Kitty's hand and smiled at Jeremy Tartal. "I'm so glad we get to explore the city together. It's going to be great sharing the experience with you!"

When Jeremy's answer got drowned out by the music, they all laughed and turned their attention back to the band. Randy Wright, Lana's fellow

Wanderlust Tours guide, burst through the crowd and plopped down in the chair next to her.

"This is going to be a good group, I think," he shouted into her ear.

Two hours ago, they had welcomed their new group of tourists to Dublin for a weeklong tour. Usually, they started off with a meal in a quiet restaurant so that the guides and guests could get to know each other a little better. Yet before they could finish their "welcome to Ireland" speech, one guest asked whether they could start off by getting a real Guinness, and another seconded the request.

Lana and Randy only had time to introduce themselves before their motley crew was heading back out on the town. Luckily their hotel's location in the heart of the city's center meant they had easy pickings of some of the best pubs in Dublin. A catchy Irish tune wafting out of an open pub door drew them in, and soon they were all drinking and dancing the night away.

"They do seem pretty comfortable here, and with each other, already," Lana replied.

Patrick, a spry eighty-two-year-old, seemed at home sitting at the long bar, where he could easily watch the podium and ensure that his drink wasn't knocked over by an enthusiastic dancer. His flaming red hair and handlebar moustache softened his stern appearance.

His equally redheaded son, Paddy, and daughter-in-law, Nina, were in the center of the tiny room dancing so close that they brought a blush to Lana's cheek. *What an odd couple—opposites really do attract*, she thought. Whereas Paddy had the broad build of a high school quarterback and dressed as if he was a corporate executive, his wife, Nina, was as petite as a ballerina and swathed in a black leather ensemble suitable for a night of clubbing. Most of all, it was the tattoos covering both of Nina's arms that didn't seem to mesh with Paddy's wholesome appearance.

A smile crossed Lana's face when Paddy scooped up his wife and twirled her around, barely missing two pints in the process. No one minded; in fact, the patrons at the surrounding tables cheered them on.

The only person who frowned was Jeanie, a fifty-three-year-old woman traveling by herself. Swaying to the rhythm on the outskirts of the dance floor, she was taking tiny sips of her pint while attempting to dance provocatively. Unfortunately, there wasn't enough room for her intended hip maneuvers, making her dance appear more like she was spinning an invisible hula-hoop around her waist.

On the walk from the hotel to the pub, Jeanie had wrapped her arm around Lana's and enthusiastically told her all about her interest in Irish history, food, and mythology. Lana got the impression that Jeanie chattered nonstop because she was traveling without a companion and was anxious. Her client also did mention that she suffered from terrible motion sickness and that this was her first time abroad in many years, which might be compounding her nervousness.

Dancing a few steps in front of Jeanie was Mitch Anders, a man also traveling without a companion. Lana briefly wondered whether he and Jeanie might be a good match, but something about his laid-back attitude and manner of dressing made her doubt that they would. His skin was so pasty white, Lana wondered whether he was allergic to the sun. He was in his mid-sixties, yet wearing clothes designed for a much younger man. His many necklaces and bracelets jangled as he clapped his hands in perfect rhythm with the musicians. Lana watched his mouth moving and realized he was singing along with the band. *How could he know this folk song?* she wondered, listening for familiar words but not finding any. *He must be passionate about Irish music*, she figured.

Suddenly Lana realized two of her clients were not dancing. She looked around the bar until she spotted Evelyn and Devon Riley in the far corner, well away from the podium. Both seemed nice enough, though quite reserved. The owner of Wanderlust Tours, Dotty Thompson, had asked her and Randy to take extra good care of them and, if they could, to find out why the Rileys had not been touring with her as often as they once had. Apparently, the couple had not been on a Wanderlust tour in almost a year, which was quite unusual considering they had booked three a year with Dotty's company since it had opened fifteen years earlier. Lana's boss was convinced that they'd had a bad experience on their last trip and were too polite to tell her. When she'd emailed to ask whether they were interested in joining this tour to Dublin, Dotty was so surprised that they said yes that she'd given them a discount as a sign of her appreciation.

Lana leaned back in her chair and observed the couple as she sipped her cider. Evelyn was watching the band, tapping her hand against the table in rhythm with the music. At least, until she noticed her husband was looking at his phone instead of the musicians. Irritation washed over her face as the couple exchanged words, resulting in Devon pocketing his phone and switching his gaze to the small podium. Evelyn grabbed his hand and swung his arm in time with the beat. When she turned to him, he gazed adoringly at his wife. However, as soon as she turned back towards the band, his smile vanished, and he stared up at the ceiling.

What is going on with those two? Lana wondered. Did Devon simply not like Irish folk music? Or were they having marital problems and using this trip to work them out? Lana truly hoped it wasn't the latter, though it wouldn't be the first time a couple had tried that trick during one of her tours. Unfortunately, it usually did not work because the stress of travel amplified the already present cracks and strains in a relationship, instead of offering the couple a chance to escape their troubles.

After the song ended and the explosion of applause died down, Kitty grabbed Lana's hand. "This is the perfect way to begin a week in Dublin!"

Jeremy wrapped an arm around his wife's shoulders and pulled her close. "It really is. Thanks again for getting us these tickets, Lana. We really needed this break."

"Gosh, Jeremy, after all you have done to help me over the years, arranging tickets for this tour was the least I could do. I swear, without your help, my mother would probably still be locked up in a Dutch prison."

"I guess we are even now," he joked.

Jeremy had been her editor when she worked as an investigative reporter for the *Seattle Chronicle*, more than a decade earlier. Over the years, he and Lana had also become good friends, and she had gotten to know his wife, Kitty, and their three children quite well.

She and Jeremy had gone through hell and back after she had been falsely accused of libel and was fired from the newspaper. Unfortunately, because

Jeremy was her editor, he also lost his job—something she had always felt personally responsible for. The only bright spot was that he had quickly found another position as editor at the *Snoqualmie Gazette*, a smaller, regional newspaper. What seemed like a step down the career ladder ultimately allowed him more free time, which made it easier to start a family. Now he and Kitty had three beautiful daughters and a lovely home on the outskirts of Seattle's city center.

When Lana had run into trouble during a few of her tours, Jeremy had kindly helped her out by using his connections and resources to discover information she ultimately used to catch a killer, including the evidence that helped free her own mother. That was something she would always be grateful to him for. When he had jokingly asked for her to arrange tickets to a Wanderlust tour as payback, Lana immediately agreed to talk to her boss. Luckily, Dotty was happy to help them out and promised to add him and his wife to the next tour that did not sell out.

"There is so much I want to see and do this week. My co-workers gave me enough suggestions to fill a month in Dublin!"

Jeremy kissed his wife's curly hair. "We'll just have to do as much as we can this week. We should enjoy our seven days of freedom to the fullest," Jeremy said with a laugh.

Jeanie, who had been leaning over to listen in, moved to a chair across from him. "That sounds mysterious. What do you mean, seven days of freedom? Are you fatally ill? Or are you going to prison?"

Jeremy sniggered, and Kitty raised an eyebrow at her. "No," he said. "We haven't been abroad since our girls were born. Being here without them does feel a little like a jailbreak."

"Hey!" When Kitty swatted his chest, he pulled his wife in close and kissed her tenderly.

Jeanie leaned forward and placed her head in between Jeremy and Kitty's, forcing the couple to detach from their embrace. "How old are your girls?"

Kitty took out her phone and brought up a lovely family photo. "Rachel is seven, Rhonda is five, and Olivia just turned two last month."

"They are gorgeous," Jeanie squealed, leaving Lana's ears ringing. "It must be tough leaving those cuties behind for a week. I don't think I could do the same. But then, I don't have kids."

Lana groaned internally at how her tour guest had unintentionally hit on a sensitive topic.

"Yes, well, we haven't taken a vacation in almost a decade, and my parents are fit enough to take care of them all," Jeremy quickly replied in a dismissive tone as a flash of concern washed over Kitty's face.

"The girls are going to be fine," he added as he squeezed her shoulder and shot a glare at Jeanie. "My parents are still in great shape; we have to grab this chance while we can," Jeremy continued when Kitty's somber expression didn't lighten. "And knowing how they like to stuff the girls full of cookies and sweets, our little angels will probably be so high on sugar the whole time, they won't even notice that we are gone."

Kitty laughed. "You do have a great point. I can imagine it's going to be difficult to get them to eat a normal breakfast, instead of ice cream, after we're back."

"That's what grandparents are for," Jeremy agreed. "And we can video chat with them every day. I already taught both my parents how to use FaceTime so we can always reach them."

Lana smiled along, glad to see Jeremy was able to salvage the mood. As much as Kitty wanted to go on vacation, Jeremy said it had taken a lot of sweet-talking to persuade his wife to come on this trip because she didn't want to be away from the girls for an entire week. However, once he convinced her it would be a waste of the plane ticket and their time to fly all the way over to Ireland for a weekend, Kitty eventually agreed. The fact that their weeklong trip was being paid for by Wanderlust Tours made it even easier to say yes.

When the band walked back towards the podium, Lana, Jeremy, Kitty, and Jeanie all turned to view them better. Something unpleasant must have caught Jeremy's eye, because he stiffened up. Lana followed his line of sight, noting that a rather small and overweight man was staring at their table. His sights seemed set on Jeremy, and his expression was anything but pleasant. Someone tapped the stranger's shoulder and motioned him forward. After a moment's hesitation, he narrowed his eyes at Jeremy once more, then walked out of the pub.

Kitty noticed Jeremy's reaction as well. "Who was that?"

Jeremy shook his head, but the puzzled frown remained. "I'm not sure. For a second, I thought I saw Guy."

"No!" Kitty gasped.

"When I told my crew where we were going on vacation, one of the reporters mentioned that Guy had recently moved over to Dublin. My mind must be playing tricks on me."

Kitty cast her eyes downward. "Why didn't you say anything? We didn't have to come to Ireland."

He raised his voice to be heard over the music. "I know you've been wanting to visit Dublin for years and were disappointed that your company didn't fly you over with the rest of the team. When Lana offered us this trip, I didn't know Guy was here. And even if I had, I still would have said yes. We are only going to be here for a few days, and it's one of the busiest weeks of the year, thanks to all the Saint Patrick's Day celebrations. What are the chances of us running into Guy this week? Maybe a million to one?"

2

Hair of the Dog

March 12—Day One of the Wanderlust Tour in Dublin, Ireland

At breakfast, most of Lana's guests were bleary eyed and holding their heads low. She was in the same boat. The incredibly large glasses made it difficult to judge how much she'd had to drink. Only later had she realized that one of those pints was equivalent to almost two of the normal beers she would have been served back in the States.

Only Patrick, their oldest guest, was chipper and alert. Was it because of the Guinness in his hand, she wondered. As if sensing her internal question, Patrick caught her eye and raised his glass. "The hair of the dog. Nothing cures a hangover better."

Lana chuckled. "I get what you mean, but I never did understand that expression."

"It's from ancient times. They thought putting the hair of the rabid dog that bit you into the wound it created would heal it faster. The theory being that like cures like. I don't know if it really works, but I'm happy to try."

He raised his glass to her before taking a large swig.

Lana's stomach jerked in revulsion; even the idea of drinking alcohol right now made her nauseated. She cast her eyes away from Patrick. "Do you need anything else?"

"I could use some more bacon and a few sausages, if you are asking," he said with a wink.

"Coming up. Paddy and Nina, can I get you two anything?"

Nina looked up at Lana, her eyes covered with large sunglasses. "A freshly squeezed orange juice would be wonderful."

"Make that two, please," Paddy whispered.

Something about Paddy's wife made Lana stop and stare. *Where do I know her face from?* Last night she'd wondered the same thing and looked up her guest's full name on the tour's itinerary. Though Nina O'Toole didn't ring any bells, Lana was still convinced that she had met the woman before. Dotty did say that all of the paying guests on this trip were regulars, so maybe she had led Nina on another tour. However, Paddy and Patrick's faces were not familiar, and Lana was fairly certain that she had never had a guest with extensive tattoos on her arms on any trip before. That was not something she would have easily forgotten.

Lana suppressed her natural curiosity, figuring it was better to give her mind a chance to mull over where she knew Nina from, before causing a potentially embarrassing situation by asking her directly. She started to walk to the breakfast bar to fulfill her guests' orders when Jeanie began flapping her arms in Lana's direction.

"Excuse me, could you get me an orange juice, too? And maybe a plate of eggs—scrambled, not sunny side up," Jeanie called out as she took the folded napkin off the table and whipped it open.

Lana bit her tongue to keep from laughing. *Oh boy, she is going to be one of those kinds of guests*, she thought. She knew from experience that some people felt the need to be treated like royalty for the duration of the tour. Lana didn't mind. If it helped her guests to enjoy their trip more, then so be it. They were paying quite a bit to be here, and the guides' sole purpose for tagging along was to ensure they had the vacation of a lifetime. Lana looked to her fellow guide, who was busy serving Devon and Evelyn their breakfast. Although he also looked worse for wear this morning, Randy was running around and cracking jokes as if he was feeling completely normal.

"Sure thing, Jeanie. Let me get the O'Tooles their breakfasts, then I'll come back with your order. Okay?"

Jeanie perked up at the name. "O'Toole? You mean to tell me that man's name is Paddy O'Toole? You can't get much more Irish than that!"

Patrick Senior scowled at her remark. "What of it?"

His gruff reaction and deep frown kept Lana's feet planted. The last thing anyone needed was a disagreement between guests at the beginning of a tour.

Jeanie rose and sat at the empty seat at the O'Tooles' table without asking. Her flowing dress billowed out behind her plump figure. She put her elbows up on the tabletop and rested her chin in her upturned palms. "Do you know where your family hailed from? Is this your first time in Ireland? How many generations ago did your ancestors emigrate to America?"

Nina smiled politely at Jeanie as Paddy placed his hand over hers and then nodded to the older gentleman at the table. "This is my wife, Nina, and my father, Patrick. Dad's father hails from Munster," Paddy said as he looked to Patrick Senior, who was staring into his Guinness. "This is our first time in Ireland, but it already feels like coming home."

His father grunted but kept his gaze focused on his beverage.

Jeanie, on the other hand, seemed to have found a soulmate. She laid her palm over Paddy's hand, startling both him and Nina. "I know what you mean. I've always wanted to celebrate Saint Patrick's name day in the old country, but my motion sickness kept me grounded. Until recently, at least." Her voice trailed off, and she released her grip on Paddy and Nina's hands.

"What made you change your mind?" Nina asked when Jeanie lapsed into silence.

Jeanie blushed and leaned away from the table, looking coyly to the ground. "A man I once loved moved here recently, and now that he's settled, I think we have a chance at making it. Circumstances drove us apart, but time heals all wounds, doesn't it? I figure if I don't come now and give us another try, I'll never know for certain."

"Good for you," Nina said. "I hope it works out for you two. Long-distance relationships are really tough to maintain. I know firsthand how hard it can be." She laid a hand on her husband's chest. "The first few years we were together, I was constantly on the road for my work. I know it put a huge strain on our relationship. But we are ultimately stronger for it."

Lana automatically thought of her boyfriend, Alex, and their relationship. Even though they lived together, both were out of the country more than they were in it. Despite the distance, they had not had any trouble keeping their romance alive.

"That's sweet of you to say," Jeanie replied. "I hope it works out, too. If you want any help researching your ancestors, I own a genealogy service and can trace most of my clients' family trees back five or six generations. Ireland is one of my specialties. If I can get back far enough, I can usually find a royal connection, as well."

Paddy's eyebrows shot up. "I don't think we have royal blood."

Jeanie said, "Until you've done all the research, you never know. That's what makes genealogy so fun—finding all of those connections to your past and personal history. Munster is a large province; I've got my laptop with me and can try to find out the name of the village he was born in, if you want. Just give me a shout, okay?"

Jeanie handed Paddy a business card and winked at him when he took it.

"AAS?" Paddy mumbled as he stared at the card.

Nina slapped his shoulder. "Watch your mouth!"

"I'm just reading her business card."

Jeanie hmphed. "My company is called Ancestors Across the Sea. Not all of us have a dirty mind."

"Thanks, but I doubt we'll need your services. After my grandfather died, I inherited a shoebox full of documents that have helped me trace the different branches of our family tree back to several towns in Munster. I know exactly where my granddad's home is because I have a copy of the deed to the property. It's right outside of Limerick and looks like a large parcel of land; I bet it's worth quite a bit."

"It never hurts to do a little more research into your past, especially if you plan on contacting your living relatives. If you give me —"

"So Paddy, it sounds like you shouldn't have any trouble finding your relatives," Lana said loudly, cutting Jeanie off in order to save the O'Tooles from another sales pitch. Her clients were on vacation, not here to be cajoled into buying products or services. Given the tour's rather expensive prices, most of their clients were quite wealthy, which made enforcing the Wanderlust Tours "no soliciting" rule an important part of the guide's responsibilities.

"Are you going to go visit your ancestral home during one of the free afternoons? If you need help arranging a ride out to the village, please let me know," Lana added.

Because this tour was a mishmash of clients' wishes, Dotty had planned several free afternoons, so that each of their guests could do the things they wanted to do most, without the rest feeling forced to go along.

"Thanks for your offer, but Nina already found a taxi company that can drive us out there for the afternoon," Paddy said and squeezed his wife's shoulder. "We booked it for March 15. I can't wait to meet my relatives and see if there are any physical similarities. We have so few pictures of Granddad's family."

"Because they kicked him out of their house and refused to answer his letters after he emigrated to America! Why would he cherish any memories of those people?" Patrick Senior asked.

"We've talked about this before," Paddy growled. Nina placed a hand on his shoulder, and her husband stared off into the distance.

"If you give me their names and dates, I can look them up in a jiffy. There might be a few photos scanned into the ancestry databases that I can access," Jeanie said, pushing herself back into the conversation.

"Why bother? I can ask to look at family photos when we go out to the house later this week."

Nina plucked the business card out of her husband's hand. "Jeanie the genealogist?"

"I was born to do the job I do!" she laughed.

"It almost sounds like the name of a band." Nina sang softly in a whiny voice, "Jeanie genealogy."

Her father-in-law frowned at her. "Nah, it doesn't have enough ring to it. Besides, I thought you were done with that trash. Did you listen to the folk CDs I lent you?"

"Yeah, Pops, I did. But it all sounds the same to me."

"I can say the same about that noise you call music," the older man grumbled.

When Nina's eyes narrowed, Lana cut into the conversation, hoping to lighten the mood. "So, Nina, Dotty tells me that you're the reason we are all here. It was your idea to make this a Saint Patrick's Day-themed trip."

Nina scowled briefly at her father-in-law before turning to Lana and nodding enthusiastically. "We had been talking about coming over for Saint Patrick's Day for years, but the timing was never right. Somehow the stars aligned this year, which is why I begged Dotty to organize something for this week. I'm so glad she was up to the challenge. And she put this tour together quite quickly, too."

Lana nodded. "It's a great idea. I'm also glad she was able to find so many clients who were able to come over at the last minute." In point of fact, Dotty used to offer a Saint Patrick's Day tour, but it had not been popular the last few years, so she took it off the schedule. When Nina inquired about putting a tour together this year, Dotty brushed off the old itinerary. Luckily, Dotty had the memory of an elephant and could still recall who had ever inquired about a trip to Ireland and contacted them all. To her delight, every couple but one was still interested and available.

Most of all, Lana was thrilled that Dotty had agreed to add Jeremy and his wife to the trip at no extra charge. She glanced over at her two friends, currently being served coffee and croissants by Randy. Despite their somewhat bleary eyes, they seemed happy and relaxed this morning. Jeremy kissed his wife's fingertips, and she giggled like a newlywed. Seeing them happy brought a smile to Lana's face, as well.

The breakfast hall door opening motivated Lana to collect the two orange juices and plate of meat for the O'Tooles. When she returned to their table, Jeanie had moved back to her original table and was staring off into space.

Mitch Anders walked over to their group. "Good morning, everyone." He nodded to the chair across from Jeanie. "Is this seat taken?"

She blushed and fluttered her eyes. "Please, be my guest."

Her reaction caught Lana off-guard. Hadn't Jeanie just told the O'Tooles that she was here to rekindle a romance with an old flame?

Mitch's long ponytail fell over his shoulder as he sat down. Unlike the rest of the group, he didn't seem to be suffering from jet lag or last night's abundance of alcohol.

"Good morning, Mitch. Did you sleep well? Can I get you something to drink or eat?" Lana asked.

"Like a baby, thanks," he said. "Could I get a bowl of fruit mixed with yogurt and a black coffee?"

"Sure thing," Lana responded, getting another throat clearing from Jeanie. "After I get Jeanie's breakfast."

"Don't forget the orange juice," the genealogist said, her tone bordering on pushy.

"Okay, be right back," Lana responded evenly, hoping her guest would lighten up a bit after she had had some breakfast. Luckily, Mitch politely complimented her colorful dress, and Jeanie's attitude softened once again. Lana chuckled to herself as she noted how Jeanie seemed to melt under Mitch's gaze. Perhaps she was working out a contingency plan, in case things didn't work out with her former lover. Lana thought back on her ex-husband and wondered how she would feel if he suddenly came back into her life and wanted to try to make their relationship work again. *No way* would be her reaction—of that, she was certain. But she was not Jeanie, and she did not know their history.

3

Holy Namesakes

After her guests were finished with their second rounds of coffees, most had perked up again and seemed to be ready to begin the day.

Before the guides could shuffle their guests to the awaiting minivan, Evelyn and Devon approached them. "Hi, Lana. Have you or Randy heard anything about Devon's luggage?"

Lana looked to her fellow tour guide, who shook his head. "No. Was it stolen?"

"No, his bag didn't make it onto our flight, so we had to fill out some paperwork after we arrived. Somehow it went to London, instead of Dublin."

"It's no big deal," Devon said. "They'll deliver it to our hotel as soon as they fly it over."

His wife seemed far more upset by the delay than he was. "But it's your first time out of the country since… I just wanted it to be perfect."

Evelyn's lip started to tremble as her husband held her tight. "Hey, come on now. We're here in Dublin together, right? Our hotel and everything else are taken care of. Besides, you wanted to go shopping while we are here. Now we have a good excuse to do so."

His response dried her eyes.

Lana was again puzzled by the Rileys' behavior. It was not the first time an airline misplaced a client's bag, but Evelyn's response was quite dramatic. "Gosh, that's really irritating," Lana said. "I haven't heard anything about your luggage yet, but I will ask the receptionists if they have heard from the airline. Alright?"

Evelyn nodded as Randy called out to their group, "Well, folks, are we ready to start our tour of Dublin?"

A round of cheers followed. Lana could tell this was going to be a good group to lead.

"We are going to start the day off with a trip to Saint Patrick's Cathedral."

"Woo-hoo, that was my request." Paddy pumped his arm in the air, as if he had won a contest.

"That's why we wanted to come to Dublin this week, to see Paddy's church and experience his namesake's special holiday in the old country," Nina enthused.

"Just because his name is Patrick does not mean Saint Patrick's Cathedral or his name day has anything to do with him. There have been Patricks in our family since I can remember!" Patrick Senior announced.

"That's not far back considering you didn't know your own granddad," Paddy countered. "That's why we're here, to rediscover our Irish roots."

"I don't understand all this fuss about finding your roots. We are as Irish as my deodorant soap," Patrick grumbled.

"How can you say that? It's as if you're ashamed of your ancestry," Jeanie scoffed.

When Patrick opened his mouth to respond, Lana butted in first. The ornery expression on the old man's face spelled trouble, and Lana wanted to begin this day on a positive note, not a sour one. "Why don't we head out to our taxi?"

Mitch waved a hand at Lana and Randy, jangling his bracelets in the process. "I do have one question. Could I get a copy of the itinerary? I asked Dotty to leave a few nights open for pub visits and want to make sure she did, before I make any plans."

Patrick slapped Mitch on the back. "We are going to get along great."

Mitch smiled gently at the older man. "I'm hoping to play during a few open sessions—that's why I brought my guitar along."

"Oh, I was hoping you wanted to sample the local brews with me. Paddy's more interested in churches and museums," Patrick muttered.

"Dad, I told you I had a surprise for you. You just have to be patient," his son counseled.

Lana blushed as she dug a stack of paper out of her bag. She had meant to give her clients copies of the new itinerary during their first meeting, but their spontaneous pub visit distracted her from doing so.

"I do apologize, folks. Here is the latest version of our itinerary." She handed the stack of papers to Mitch, who then passed them along.

"Because we wanted to include as many of your requests as we could, it took us a little longer to work out the details. There are events related to Saint Patrick's Day happening all week here in Dublin, which means most of the major tourist sites are busier than usual. That is why the first three days of our tour are quite action packed, but the last four days include trips outside of the city and more blocks of free time. We have dinner reservations most nights, but no excursions booked in the evenings. The nights are ours to explore Dublin's nightlife, or play some music," Lana finished with a nod to Mitch.

Her guests scanned their copies as they shuffled outside.

"Yes!" Paddy exclaimed. "We have VIP passes to the Saint Patrick's Day parade grandstand so we won't have to wait in the cold and rain. I knew Dotty would come through." He pulled his wife close and bent down to kiss her. "Thanks again for convincing her to set this tour up."

"Anything for you, babe." Nina beamed up at him.

A large minivan was waiting outside their hotel, situated a block from Saint Stephen's Green. As Lana helped her guests step in, drops of rain trickled down her neck. She pulled her collar up and jumped in, moments before the heavens opened up. Their taxi set off through the heart of Dublin, driving down twisting streets lined with plastered brick buildings painted in a rainbow of hues.

"Look at those adorable buildings! I've never seen so many painted in bright colors like that. It's even more charming than I envisioned," Kitty squealed as she pressed her face up against the window, seemingly oblivious to the sudden rainstorm. Jeremy leaned over his wife's shoulder and took in the sights with her, a big smile plastered on his face.

Lana understood Kitty's enthusiasm. It was the same way she felt when she arrived in Budapest for her first tour. Everything seemed to be more incredible the first time. She still loved each and every tour she had led, but the surge of newness had worn off long ago.

Their shuttle bus whipped through the streets of the city center as if the driver was trying to win a competition. Lana wished he would slow down a little so they could see the sights a bit better, as well as to ensure the safety of the many pedestrians, double-decker buses, and cyclists navigating the same narrow stretches of cobblestone and concrete.

When they turned onto a side street, their taxi drove along a magnificent stone building that spanned several blocks, with a wide turret rising out of the middle.

"Is that Dublin Castle?" Kitty exclaimed as they rounded a corner so quickly, Lana was certain they'd drifted around it.

"I think so," Randy offered as he looked to Lana. She pulled a grimace and shrugged, then grabbed her guidebook. Neither of them had been to Dublin before, and she didn't want to assume anything.

Kitty also grabbed her guidebook and tore through it, finding the section on the castle faster than Lana. "It is the castle! I'm so glad we bought this before we flew over. It was built in the 930s by Danish Vikings and was converted into a Norman fort in the twelfth century…"

"Did you say Vikings?" Jeanie asked from the back seat.

"Yes, Vikings established a settlement known as Dyflinn in the seventh century. But they were defeated by the Irish king of Midhe four years later," Kitty read aloud.

Lana thought her enthusiasm was infectious and endearing. Unfortunately, not all of her clients agreed.

"She isn't the only one with a guidebook. We can read up on the castle ourselves, if we wanted to know more about it," Paddy grumbled to his wife. Unfortunately, his complaint was easily heard by everyone in the rather small minivan.

Kitty's eyes widened to saucers as she stammered, "Oh, gosh, I'm sorry. I didn't mean to bother you…" Her voice trailed off as she dropped her head and leaned back into her seat.

Nina's expression grew grim as she shot her husband the evil eye, then leaned over the seat to pat Kitty on the shoulder. "Don't you worry about it. It was interesting to learn more about what we are seeing. I'm afraid we are both a little cranky. Neither one of us got much sleep on the plane and we drank too much last night, so we're pretty worn out."

"They bumped us from down from first class to business class," Paddy grumbled.

"Because you didn't have as many frequent-flyer miles as you thought you did and refused to pay the extra fees," Nina explained. From her exasperated tone, it was clearly not for the first time.

"We did save some money, but it was so cramped back there," Paddy whined.

"We'll just have to upgrade our tickets for the ride back, no matter what the cost," Nina reasoned. "Luckily for Paddy I'm tiny enough that he could squeeze over onto my seat, as well."

Patrick rolled his eyes. "What a waste of money. Was it so terrible, having to associate with normal people? I thought it was pretty darn comfortable."

His remarks echoed Lana's sentiment, though she did wonder whether he was baiting his son again. It seemed to be Patrick's favorite pastime.

"Excellent. We don't have to upgrade your seat if you don't want to fly first class," Nina retorted.

Her reply shut her father-in-law right up.

Kitty's expression softened. "I couldn't sleep either. Luckily, Jeanie had some Dramamine so I spared myself the embarrassment of getting sick on the plane, as well. Though it wasn't just the motion sickness that kept me up. We haven't been on vacation in years and several of my co-workers were just here, so they got me all excited to visit. I guess their enthusiasm is fueling mine right now."

"Who do you work for?" Paddy asked.

"Firehouse Brewery. It's a microbrewery based out of Fremont."

"I love your beer! We stock your ales in my clubs," Nina said.

Did she mean nightclubs? Lana thought, wondering whether that was how they'd met. When she was in Seattle, one of her favorite pastimes was going out to listen to live music.

"Two of our pale ales recently won gold and silver at a national craft brewery competition," Kitty said with pride. "Personally, I think our newest amber ale is one of the best I've ever tasted."

"Since Kitty started working there six months ago, she has become obsessed with trying as many varieties as she can. She has become quite the beer connoisseur," Jeremy laughed.

"Save yourself the trouble. Yours are some of the best craft beers in the Pacific Northwest," Patrick said. "Firehouse Blonde is my favorite. It is a shame your microbrewery is getting bought up by EuroBeer."

Kitty frowned at the older man. "No, they aren't buying us out. It's a merger. Our boss has arranged for our job security in the deal. They just want to distribute our recipes in Europe."

Patrick shrugged. "I must have read the article wrong. But you watch out for what bosses say, especially when they have a financial interest. I hope for your sake he's not a liar. That's how I got made redundant. Management kept telling us that it was a merger, but when it turned out to be an acquisition, almost all of us lost our jobs. I received a pretty crappy severance package as thanks for a lifetime of work."

Kitty shook her head resolutely. "No, our boss promised us that we would all keep our jobs. EuroBeer wants to distribute our beers in Europe, that's all. It's cheaper for us to work with them, instead of trying to establish our own distribution channels. Craft breweries are now outselling the larger brands, which is why most of the international brewers are aligning themselves with regional ones. Besides, most of the staff have worked for Firehouse since it started ten years ago. I can't imagine the owners would lie to them."

"Greed does funny things to a person. Watch out, is all I'm saying."

Kitty's previous enthusiasm had faded considerably, and her mouth formed a pencil-thin line.

Nina leaned forward. "Why were your co-workers here recently and you were not?"

"Most of my department flew over to discuss the merger, but I wasn't important enough to join them," Kitty laughed. "But their stories made me want to come. Jeremy and I love history and literature, and Dublin's got plenty of both."

"Don't forget the beer!" Jeremy said, getting a cheer out of Patrick and Paddy.

4

Tricksters in Green

They crossed the tiny center in mere minutes, yet Lana was glad for the ride. The busy traffic meant they had a dry place from which to view the city's colorful architecture on the rainy drive over. As the thunderclouds opened up, her group raced inside the cathedral and shook off the thick drops of rain covering their hats, scarves, and jackets. Fortunately, Dotty had warned her group and guides to dress in layers and be prepared for lots of precipitation. March in Ireland was still very much the rainy season, and cold to boot. *Finally, some place in the world with more rain than Seattle*, Lana thought, recalling all of the jokes Seattleites suffered as residents of one of the rainiest places in the United States.

Mitch held the door open for Jeanie, who beamed as she bowed regally, as if she expected such treatment. Lana was glad there was a single man for her to focus her attention on, though she did think it was a peculiar way to act, given Jeanie was here to reunite with her former lover.

As the O'Tooles passed, the way Nina smiled up at her husband niggled at her brain. She had definitely met her before, but where and when? It was starting to drive Lana a bit batty. If she couldn't figure it out soon, she would have to ask.

She and Randy brought up the rear, closing the door just as a flash of lightning lit up the stained-glass windows. The resulting clap of thunder boomed through the vast cathedral. As they entered the church's nave, Lana's eyes automatically drifted upwards towards the impossibly high ceiling. The solid structure didn't sway or creak as the storm raged on outside. It was somewhat magical being inside this massive enclosed space with the thunder and lightning crashing down outside.

Lana was so entranced with the dance of light created by the colored glass on the stone walls and statues that she didn't notice the young man approaching from behind.

"Welcome to Saint Patrick's Cathedral. Are you the Wanderlust Tours group, then?" a delightful accent asked.

Lana turned to see a blond man with bushy eyebrows smiling up at them. "Yes, we are, thank you. Good to meet you."

The young man turned to her clients. "Welcome to Saint Patrick's, the largest cathedral in Ireland and our national church. It is said that Saint Patrick used a well on this site to baptize Christian converts over fifteen hundred years ago. The current building was originally constructed between 1220 and 1260; however, it has undergone many a renovation since then, including one funded by the Guinness family in 1860."

Patrick Senior nodded in appreciation. "I knew they were good people."

In the young man's mouth, "that" became "dat" and "a" sounded more like "ah" to her. Lana reveled in the man's accent, enjoying how he stretched his words in a lyrical way.

"It's like coming home," Paddy said as he gazed around the massive church with a content smile on his face.

"Are you Catholic?"

Paddy looked at the young man as if he was crazy. "No, my name is Patrick."

The guide's bushy eyebrows shot up as he waited for Paddy to explain. However, Lana's guest remained silent.

When Patrick Senior sniggered, Nina shot her father-in-law a nasty look. "Because my husband's name is Patrick, he feels like this is his namesake's church," Nina explained as she laid her hand on her husband's chest. "He's been looking forward to coming here for years."

The guide beamed up at him. "That's a right good name to have. Are you staying in town for the Saint Patrick's Day parade?"

"You better believe it. If you are going to visit Dublin, it might as well be during the best holiday in the world."

"True. Come, let us explore your cathedral."

Nina smiled warmly at their guide for playing along, then gazed lovingly up at her husband. Paddy glowed as he stepped in line behind the young Irishman. Patrick Senior shook his head slightly as he waited for the rest to pass.

Lana slid up next to him. "You don't seem as proud of your namesake as your son."

"Patrick is one of the most popular names in the world—whether you are Irish or not. It's not like we named him after the saint; we were simply following tradition. My great-great-grandfather was the first Patrick in our family, and since then all of the first male children have gotten stuck with it. I guess it's a good thing Paddy didn't have a son, otherwise it would have continued."

"Do he and Nina have children?"

"Five girls."

"Phew, that's a handful," Lana responded automatically, before her hand flew in front of her face, embarrassed by what she'd said.

"Yeah, well, nannies come in handy when both parents work."

"What does Nina do? She looks so familiar."

"Nothing worth writing home about. If you really want to know, ask her yourself." Patrick scowled as he slowed his pace even further, clearly done talking to her. "I'm going to sit here on this pew. I don't need to hear that boy's talk; I can see enough from here."

"Are you certain?"

"I'm eighty-two years old. Trust me, I've seen enough churches and had enough history lessons to last me a lifetime."

"Oh, okay. We will come get you when we are finished with the tour."

Patrick grunted and looked up at the ceiling. Lana followed suit, briefly astounded by the impossibly high arches before sprinting over to her group, now entering the Lady Chapel. She caught up with them as their guide was finishing his softly spoken explanation of the gorgeous chapel's history and current use as a baptismal site.

The long rectangular space was a forest of stone arches and stained-glass windows perfectly framing a stone altar. Lana was captivated by the heavenly blue light dancing across the many pillars and spilling over the mosaic floors.

"It's so beautiful," Jeanie whispered as she took a picture. When the flash went off, she cried out, "Oh, gosh, I'm so sorry!" Several worshippers and tourists looked to see what the commotion was as Jeanie began berating herself. "I can delete it if you want. But that won't save your glorious artifacts from my flash's light burst. How could I be so stupid?"

Jeanie's extreme reaction to a simple mistake puzzled Lana. Was she truly so sensitive, or was she hunting for a little extra male attention? When the young man smiled and laughed, Jeanie immediately began batting her eyes at him. Lana rolled hers, wondering whether that story about meeting up with her former lover was true at all.

The young guide patted her hand as if he was comforting his grandmother. "Saint Patrick's has survived multiple fires, its tower being blown down, and the suppression of Edward VI. I think it can handle a camera flash now and again."

When he turned and began walking back into the main cathedral, Jeanie followed him like a faithful puppy dog. The rest followed suit, except for the Rileys. Evelyn was studying the stained glass, pointing out different details to her husband. Devon, on the other hand, seemed indifferent to her remarks or the beautiful windows.

It would not be the first time on one of Lana's tours that one half of a couple was more interested in the sites than the other one was. However, Evelyn was clearly displeased. That, in Lana's mind, could be problematic, especially if Evelyn could not leave Devon be. Her heart went out to the couple. *Their marital troubles must be why they haven't been on vacation in a year*, she thought. Dotty would be sad to learn the truth. From what she had told Lana, both were normally chatterboxes who were a delight to have on tour.

She slowly walked over to them, wondering whether it was better to let them be. However, she didn't want her guests to think that they had left without them. "Pardon me, the tour is moving on, but we don't want to rush you. Would you like to stay here a bit longer? These windows are incredible."

"No, that's okay. We can stick with the tour. Right, Evelyn?" Devon said as he began walking towards the chapel's entrance.

Evelyn blew out her cheeks. "Is there nothing in this world that interests you anymore?"

Devon turned and narrowed his eyes at his wife. "Thank you, Lana, for letting us know. We will catch up with you in a minute."

Lana scurried out of the chapel, hoping that her guests could work out their differences, if not completely, then at least enough that they wouldn't spoil the tour for the rest of the participants.

Randy waved her over to their group, now circling their guide and staring down at the floor at the west end of the church. She passed the choir decorated with ancient flags and knights' helmets to reach them, marveling at the captivating sculptural decorations as she went. When she got closer, Lana noticed they were staring at several gravestones set in the floor close to a wall filled with sculptured busts and plaques. A highly polished gold plaque caught Lana's eye. On it was the word "Swift" in large gothic letters, followed by "Decan 1713, 19 Oct 1745."

As she caught up, their guide was pointing around the space. "Many of Ireland's most important citizens are buried here," he explained to her group.

"Then I suspect one of my ancestors is here, among the dead," Jeanie said before clapping her hands together. The sudden noise in this quiet cathedral made many heads turn.

"You don't say! What is your family name? We have a chart of the burial plots that I can consult for you."

Jeanie laughed heartily. "Honestly, I don't know their name yet, but I am certain one of my ancestors was a famous Irishman. Maybe a wealthy landowner, writer, or even royalty. I just need to go back further in time to discover which one it is. That's what I'm here to find out. I expect by the time this week is over, there will be reason to call me Lady Jeanie."

The guide bowed deeply. "May your ancestor be rich and famous. With a little luck, you will be related to the most renowned person buried within our walls—Jonathan Swift. He was a dean of this cathedral and also a well-known author. Two of his death masks, a cast of his skull, and some of his early writings are also on display here."

Jeanie's smiled faded as the guide moved on with his repertoire, clearly not interested in learning more about her suspicions or assumptions.

"Are you kidding me? This is Jonathan Swift's grave?" Kitty exclaimed.

"I wouldn't joke about such a thing," the young man said.

Kitty squeezed Jeremy's arm. "We knew that he was Irish, but we didn't know he was once a dean of this cathedral or that he is buried here. Oh, Lana, can you take a picture of us with his tombstone?"

She did as her friends asked, then cast her eyes down towards his gravestone and snapped another picture of the gold-plated memorial. "Who is Jonathan Swift?"

"The author of *Gulliver's Travels*. Oh! This would be a perfect article for your blog! Are you still writing posts?"

Lana reddened. "To be honest, I've been lagging behind these past few months, because of working all of the extra tours. I think I read *Gulliver's Travels* during high school, but I don't really remember the story."

"It was one of my favorite books when I was a teenager," Kitty said. "And we found a children's version that our girls just love us to read to them before bedtime."

"It really does capture the sense of adventure and wonder of the original story, without us having to explain the political satire," Jeremy added, then looked around the vast cathedral. "I wonder if they have a copy of it in their gift shop."

"Yes, we do have several versions, including illustrated ones," the guide chimed in. "I'll walk you over to the gift shop after the tour is finished. It is a wonderful story, beloved by young and old. And don't worry; you are not the first person to be surprised that Jonathan Swift was dean of a church in Dublin. I'm impressed you knew that he was an Irishman; most foreigners only think of shamrocks, leprechauns, and Oscar Wilde when they think of Ireland."

"I thought Oscar Wilde was Scottish," Jeanie mumbled.

A pained look crossed their guide's face, though he quickly regained his composure.

"Truth be told, our girls love leprechauns as much as they do *Gulliver's Travels*. I've often wondered if those creatures inspired his Lilliputians," Kitty said.

Their guide nodded thoughtfully. "There are many that would agree with you. His Lilliputians are also naughty little fairies and do love to cause all sorts of mischief."

"I always thought leprechauns were okay as long as you didn't try to steal their gold," Jeanie replied. Lana squinted at her guest, wondering whether she was joking.

"No, you'd best be wary of any leprechauns crossing your path," their guide responded in a most serious tone. "They are mighty tricksters, they are."

Jeanie's mouth formed a strange O, as if she was not entirely certain whether their guide was pulling her leg. However, before she could respond, the young man turned on his heel and headed towards the gift shop.

5

Tap Dancing Seagulls

When they exited the church, the sun was shining and birds were singing. A few puddles were the only signs that a rainstorm had recently occurred. Even the park benches they passed seemed to be drying rapidly, Lana noted as she and Randy checked the street names before leading their group to their next destination.

"Who is hungry?" Randy asked, getting a chorus of affirmative reactions. "Excellent. We have a special treat for you that is only a few blocks away. It's one of Dublin's must-eats—and one of the oldest restaurants in the city!"

Randy's gusto worked its magic, as it always did. He was truly the most positive person Lana had ever met, and she knew she could always count on him to keep the group spirit up. As they crossed through Saint Patrick's Park and then out onto a long street filled with shops, Lana listened as her group jubilantly discussed the history of the church and the famous corpses buried under its floor.

On the way, Lana noticed Evelyn take her husband's arm and point out several pretty architectural details and public artworks as they passed by. Her client seemed to appreciate art and architecture, yet her husband's response did not come close to matching her level of enthusiasm.

Lana sped up a little to catch up with Jeremy and Kitty, both animatedly discussing James Joyce and Oscar Wilde's contributions to literature. She had read both authors' works but wasn't enough of a fan to recall any of the texts well enough to debate their styles or literary merit. She hung back and listened, when Jeremy suddenly froze and turned pale.

"That couldn't be..."

Kitty stopped as well, following his gaze across the street. Lana looked, too, but only saw a plethora of shoppers and a few groups of tourists walking past.

"What's wrong?" Kitty asked.

"I swear I saw Guy pass by," he mumbled.

Lana's ears perked up; this was the second time they had mentioned that name.

Kitty clicked her tongue. "Come on, Jeremy. I have seen plenty of heavyset men here that resemble Guy. I seriously doubt it was him."

"Maybe."

From Jeremy's brooding expression, it was clear to Lana that he didn't agree with his wife. "Who is Guy and why do you not want to run into him?"

Both Kitty and Jeremy flinched.

"Oh, gosh, I didn't see you there, Lana. It's nothing. Kitty's right—my mind must be playing tricks on me. Guy and I had a falling-out a few months ago, and I would rather not run into him. That's all." Jeremy chuckled, but Lana could still hear the stress in his voice.

"I'm sure it was a local," Kitty said, her tone making clear that the topic was closed.

Before Lana could press her friend for details, Patrick called out, "Do we have time for a beer?" The old man pointed at a sign leading to the Guinness Storehouse.

"We have reservations for their Ambassador Experience in two days. It's a guided tour, and you get to learn how to pull your own pint!"

"I don't want to learn how to pour one, I want to drink one!"

Patrick's single-minded focus on drinking was starting to get on Lana's nerves, but she kept her voice calm. "Right now, we need to eat some lunch, then get to Trinity College for our reserved time slot. It's Dublin's most popular tourist attraction, and I would hate for you to miss it. Frankly, we are lucky we were able to get entrance tickets at all. With this being Saint

Patrick's week, the city is busier than normal, and almost everything was booked out during the last days of our trip."

When Patrick began to grouse again, Lana turned away so as to ignore him better and noticed a long line of people stretching before them on the sidewalk. It was leading towards a small shop with a green and gold sign proclaiming it to be Leo Burdock Famous Fish & Chips Since 1913. "Dublin's Oldest Chipper" was printed onto its awning.

"Hey, gang, we are here," Lana called out as she pointed towards the sign. According to Dotty, and pretty much every guidebook Lana had read, fish 'n' chips at Leo Burdock's was a must-eat experience. The wall of fame hanging on the outside wall of the shop, showcasing visits from celebrities and politicians from around the world enjoying their meal, attested to that fact. Which made it surprising to see that the shop really was more takeaway than eat in—they only had three tiny tables available and a line of tourists wanting to sit there, even for a few minutes.

Randy kept an eye on the guests while Lana ordered cod and chip combinations for them all. Luckily, Leo Burdock's staff was apparently used to prepping multiple orders simultaneously. Soon the young men working behind the tiny counter were scooping a thick layer of french fries and a large fillet of fish into each takeaway box. After a short wait, she carried the bags filled with eleven orders back out to her group. The aroma of salty fish and greasy chips were making her salivate.

"Okay, gang, our next stop is Trinity College, which is a short walk thataway," Lana said as she nodded to her right. "We are going to pass Dubh Linn Park on the way, and I thought we could find some benches to sit on while we eat our lunch. It's part of the Dublin Castle complex, but is free to enter. The views are quite incredible," Lana said, her tone self-assured despite the fact that she had never before visited the park or city.

"Why couldn't we have gone to a proper restaurant with tables and chairs?" Patrick Senior grumbled from the rear. "Nina said this trip cost a lot. If this tour is so fancy, why are we eating takeaway?"

Nina rolled her eyes and whispered something to her husband, getting a wicked grin in response.

Lana hoped the older man was simply having trouble from jet lag; otherwise this was going to be a long week. "Fish and chips at Leo Burdock's is a tradition here in Dublin, and we didn't want you to miss it. It is too bad that they don't have a larger dining area, but as you already noted, this lunch is all wrapped up to go. I'm happy to take you back to the hotel, if you prefer, while Randy leads the rest to the park. You can eat your lunch in your room and then perhaps take a nap. I would hate to tire you out on the first day." She smiled broadly, hoping to take the edge off of her remark. She didn't want to offend Patrick, but she didn't want him to ruin their lunch, either.

"I'll have enough time to sleep when I'm dead," he growled and pushed forward to the front of the group.

Nina slid up to Lana and whispered, "The fresh air will do him good. Try to ignore him, if you can. Trust me, I know it's hard to do. He's a good guy, deep down. Being made redundant was the start of several bad years that left him pretty bitter. I honestly don't know why he insisted he come on this trip; he hates Ireland and always said he never wanted to visit. That's probably why my Paddy is almost obsessed with his Irish roots."

"Maybe Patrick realized it was one of his last chances to visit? He is eighty-two, and travel does take quite a bit out of you. The older you get, the harder it is," Lana offered, feeling a tinge of sympathy for the older man. "I know I've had to send back at least a dozen clients who thought they were healthy enough to keep up with the group, but just couldn't do it. It's frustrating to travel a long distance and then not be able to do anything but hang around a hotel while you're there."

"Perhaps. Though I suspect he came along to ruin the trip for Paddy. Pops has always made fun of Paddy's interest in his ancestry." Nina's eyes hardened as she looked to her father-in-law. "I was hoping this trip might reignite Patrick's interest in their family's history, but now I'm not so sure."

"I heard Paddy mention he had inherited a box of paperwork from his grandfather. That must have given him a lot of leads into his lineage," Lana said.

Nina nodded enthusiastically. "It was the starting point. Luckily, Paddy was able to go through his grandfather's house after he died, before his father had everything removed by a cleaning company. From what my husband said, Pops didn't want to save anything."

"Wow, Patrick and his father must have had a horrible relationship."

"That's the thing, they got along quite well. But his dad hated Ireland and refused to talk about his extended family. All we know for certain is that his parents kicked him out when he was seventeen and that he never forgave them. And Patrick is the least sentimental man I have ever met and seems to loathe anything to do with the past. Since his dad died five months ago, I haven't heard him mention him once, even though he used to visit him every week."

"That is odd. But maybe it is his way of dealing with his grief?"

"I guess. I do wonder how my Paddy is going to react, when Patrick finally kicks the bucket."

"Dubh Linn Park is on your right. I see a few empty benches close to the entrance; let's lead our group over there," Randy said in a soft voice as he passed behind Lana. She was surprised to see that they were already at the park. The city center was much smaller than she had anticipated.

They entered a passageway leading through the base of the castle and into a public park. Before them was a massive circle of empty space, filled only by grass. Encircling the green was a narrow cobblestone path and several park benches. Curiously, a pattern had been set into the soft grass, its curved lines filling the circular space. In between the loops of thin stone sat students on blankets reveling in the unexpected burst of sunshine.

When her group stepped further into the enclosure, Lana looked back and immediately asked her guests to do the same. The view of the castle complex was incredible. The massive turret in its middle seemed to sprout out of the series of stone structures. On its right stood the castle's church, and on its left, stately offices and residences. Buildings painted in salmon and white circled the garden, contrasting nicely with the gray stone of the castle walls.

"We have a serving of fish and chips for everyone, and there are enough empty park benches for all of us," Randy called out to the group. "Should we spread out over there?"

Their guests wandered to where he was pointing and took over four park benches set close together. Only the Rileys remained standing in the entryway. Evelyn seemed to be staring at the pattern etched into the circular space.

Lana took two portions of fish and chips over to the couple, hoping that she wouldn't have to continually coax them into taking part in the group activities and meals.

"Did you notice it, too, Devon?" Evelyn pointed to the curved lines set in the grass. Her eyes sparkled, and a smile tugged at her lips.

"Is everything alright?" Lana asked, but neither seemed to hear her.

Devon was examining the pattern, but didn't seem as captivated by it as his wife was. "Oh yeah, the designs in the grass are Celtic. Clever."

Evelyn's eyebrows knitted together. "It's the same design as on our rings. Do you honestly not see it?"

"Huh, you're right. It is the same pattern as the rings that were stolen. That's interesting," Devon said. Yet from his tone, he didn't sound interested in the slightest.

"Come on, Devon. Can't even pretend to be interested in something? Anything—I don't care what. It's like you are dead inside, and I don't want to live with a corpse!" Evelyn cried. When she noticed Lana standing close by, she shielded her face and scurried behind her husband.

Devon took their portions of fish and chips from Lana's hand. "Thanks for lunch. We will join you in a minute."

As Lana turned towards the others, Devon tentatively wrapped his arms around his wife. "You are right, I'll try harder. I shouldn't let my business affect our relationship this much. It's just that I feel so worthless. It's hard to be interested in anything anymore."

Evelyn pushed her face into his chest and began sobbing.

Lana couldn't help but drag her feet a little, wondering what was upsetting Evelyn so. Was it merely that Devon was not as interested in this trip as she was? Lana had learned over time that not everyone appreciated the same excursions or tourist attractions as their partners did. That disconnect could sometimes create tensions, but Evelyn's reaction was pretty extreme.

Lana sat down next to Randy and dug into her takeaway, finishing her fish and most of her chips in record time. The salty treat was heavenly. Uncharacteristically, Randy was less quick; by the time Lana had thrown away her empty box, he was still busy with his meal.

When she plopped back down next to her fellow guide, his hand was frozen halfway to his mouth, and he seemed to be gazing off into the distance.

"Are you doing alright, Randy? You seem a bit preoccupied today." In fact, Randy had seemed distracted during the past two tours they had led together, but whenever she asked him about it, he brightened up and said it was nothing.

He stifled a yawn with the back of his hand. "I'm just a little worn out, that's all. When Gloria called last night, we got to talking about what color carpet and wall paint she should buy. It's rough not being there to help get our new condo ready to live in, and she's getting sick of dealing with all the renovation work herself. I don't blame her—it was my idea to buy a fixer-upper." He shook his head and sighed. "Before I knew it, it was three in the morning and we still hadn't agreed on a color scheme."

"Ouch, that was a late night." Lana cringed, knowing that he was having trouble balancing the pressures of adjusting to his new married life. It didn't help that he had been abroad for most of the three months they had been wedded. Their boss, Dotty, hadn't intentionally scheduled him to be away more than usual. Unfortunately for him, they were short a few guides, and all of their tours were sold out. Luckily, he and Lana had been working the last two tours together, and they knew each other so well now, they hardly had to talk about any issues that arose—a nod or nudge was often enough.

When Randy remained silent, Lana asked, "Did you have a chance to read through the entire itinerary and tour notes for today? After lunch, we are walking over to Trinity College."

"To see the Book of Kells, at Evelyn's request," Randy finished. "Don't worry—I am not so tired that I cannot do my job. I won't leave you hanging."

"Trust me, I know you won't—you are a great guide. But it's got to be difficult for you, being so far away from your new wife."

"Since we got married, I've been on the road more than at home. I know it's been like that for most of our relationship, but it feels different now that we've decided to commit our lives to each other. I miss her more than I did when we were just girlfriend and boyfriend."

Lana felt her throat tightening. Randy wasn't only a fellow guide; he was also the first one she trained, and they had become quite close since he joined Wanderlust Tours a year earlier—even more so since she started dating his older brother, Alex.

The alarm beeping on her phone interrupted their heart-to-heart. "To be continued," she sighed. "I'm so sorry, Randy, but we have to round up our guests and get them to Trinity College."

Lana looked to her group. Birds danced at their feet, waiting for one of them to drop a chip or chunk of fish, but she didn't see anyone still busy eating their lunch. Even Devon and Evelyn appeared to be done with their meals.

"Our time slot starts in thirty minutes. It's only a few minutes' walk, but through a pretty part of town, so we can see more of the city on the way over. Why don't we round up the garbage and then motivate them to get moving?"

"Sounds like a plan," Randy said and charged forward towards the closest guest. Jeanie was sitting alone on a park bench. Next to her was her portion, half eaten. A large seagull was tap dancing its way over to her leftover fish when Randy approached and spooked it off.

"Are you finished with that?" he asked.

"Oh yes, it was too much for me. Please do take it away," Jeanie said.

The garbage can was only two steps away from her guest. Lana chuckled internally; Jeanie really did expect the royal treatment.

Before Randy could grab her uneaten portion, the seagull swooped up and grabbed a large piece of fish. Randy waved his hands at the bird, shooing it away from the rest of the leftovers, causing the seagull to fly off, low over their group. A chunk of fish covered in tartar sauce broke free from the bird's steal and fell onto Paddy's head.

"What the!" When he jerked up, the fish slid down his cheek and landed on his shoulder. "Eew!"

Nina flicked off the food and began wiping at the smeared tartar sauce running down her husband's face and shirt.

"You're ruining his shirt!" Jeanie shrieked, as she pranced over and snatched the napkin out of Nina's hand. "You have to dab at it, not rub it. Otherwise, you're just smearing it into the fabric."

Jeanie fervently dabbed at Paddy's shirt, scowling at the yellowish stain. "Lana, can you get me a vinegar?" she snapped with the intensity of an emergency room nurse. "Someone is bound to have an extra portion they didn't use up."

Paddy and Nina were frozen in place, both with their eyes wide and mouths hanging open.

Lana looked through their leftovers and fished out a packet of white vinegar. She handed Jeanie the sauce, almost afraid to not follow her orders. Jeanie ripped it open and smeared it into the fabric before Paddy could react.

"Just hold on a minute—" he said and began to rise.

Jeanie pushed him back down onto the bench. "It's an expensive shirt. It would be a waste not to rescue it while you still can. Once the tartar sauce dries, it'll set in the fabric and be a whole lot more difficult to get out," she explained as she dabbed at the vinegar. Moments later, she stepped back and examined her work.

Lana was impressed; the stain was no longer yellow.

"There. It looks like I got all of the oil out," Jeanie said in a satisfied tone. "It's the mayonnaise that makes it tough to remove completely." She looked at Paddy's cheek and frowned. "That just leaves your face."

She spit onto the napkin and moved in towards Paddy's cheek, who jerked back and sprung off the bench before she could touch him. He held up his palms, blocking her from getting closer.

"Thanks for the tip, but I can do it myself."

"Your choice." Jeanie shrugged and handed the napkin back to Nina, who promptly threw the spit-covered cloth into the nearest garbage bin.

"Nobody appreciates help these days," Lana heard Jeanie grumble as she stepped away from the couple and crossed her arms over her ample torso.

6

Book of Kells

"What is this place?" Nina whispered to her husband.

"I don't know, but it looks really old."

Lana nodded in agreement. Entering the gates of Trinity College was akin to stepping back in time. Several regal buildings fashioned out of a light gray stone were situated around a massive cobblestoned courtyard. Most were topped by thick brick chimney stacks, and their entrances were hidden behind a forest of pillars. A campanile, a small stone structure with a domed roof topped with a cross, stood on the cusp of a field of grass that was dotted with gleaming white statues.

"This is Ireland's oldest university and has educated well-known Irishmen such as Bram Stoker, Oscar Wilde, and Jonathan Swift," Lana called out to her group, who were spreading out across the courtyard. She dared not say more because Dotty had warned her that private tours were not allowed. Unfortunately for her group, all of the official tours had already been booked up for the week. Luckily, the Book of Kells was displayed in the college's library and was accessible without having to join a tour.

"What an incredibly posh university," Nina said.

"I can only imagine how much a year would cost here," Jeanie said as she marveled at the massive buildings.

She and Randy gave their clients a moment to soak up the atmosphere and snap a few photos before steering them towards the entrance to the exhibition they had come here to see.

After waiting in a long line, their group was finally ushered inside. They first walked through an exhibition that used texts, paintings, drawings, and prints of old Celtic passages from the Book of Kells to explain its cultural and historical significance. The book was in fact an illustrated version of the first four books of the New Testament, created by monks in the ninth century. Lana particularly enjoyed the photos explaining how the letters were turned into tiny works of art.

Evelyn was the only one lingering over the descriptions when it was her group's turn to enter the Treasury, the room where the book's actual pages were displayed. The smallness of the space warranted a limited number of visitors, meaning they only had a few minutes to view the book before being ushered back out. A sign noted that only two pages were displayed at a time because they were so delicate, they couldn't be exposed to light for long periods of time without being damaged.

As soon as the door opened, Evelyn was at the front, pulling her husband along with her. Lana smiled and stepped aside, knowing this was Evelyn's top choice of things to do while they were in Dublin.

"It's even more beautiful than I had imagined. Look at the richness of the color! And the detailing of the letters and scrollwork," Evelyn exclaimed as she stuck her nose close to the glass and examined the displayed pages intently.

Unfortunately for Evelyn, her husband did not seem very interested in the pages. After a few seconds of hovering over the glass, Devon stepped away so to give another a chance to view it.

Lana leaned in to catch a quick glimpse of the book before stepping to the back of the group. The highly decorated pages featured mythical beasts and an angel playing a harp, along with a thick Gothic text written in Latin. The colors were so bright and crisp, it could have been painted a week earlier. Many of the letters had been filled in with a yellowy gold color, and delicate flowers had been added between some of the words, as if to mark the end of a sentence. It was quite beautiful, Lana thought, surprised to be so entranced by the delicate pages and drawings.

Evelyn pointed to the image of a monk seemingly hiding behind the letter *H* and asked, "Devon, did you see this detailing?"

"That's delightful." He rocked back on his heels and glanced around the room.

"What is wrong with you?" Evelyn hissed. "A year ago you would have lectured me on the craftsmanship and symbology, but now you can't even be bothered to look? This is the high point of medieval art!"

"You know perfectly well what's wrong—" he replied, then glanced around as if he'd suddenly remembered that they were not alone. He stepped towards the corner of the room, but it made little difference in this small space. "Nobody cares what I think about anything anymore. Art just doesn't thrill me like it used to."

Evelyn threw her hands on her hips. "That is ridiculous! You spent your life studying and collecting beautiful things, and now you can't be bothered to look? It's not a switch you throw on or off."

Devon shrugged, seemingly indifferent to her emotional state. "It's rather difficult to look back fondly on my career considering how things ended."

"You can still appeal the last ruling. Our lawyer thinks you have a shot at winning this time," Evelyn whispered in a fervent tone.

"That reporter refused to divulge his sources or share his notes. Until he does, we won't stand a chance."

"Of course he won't disclose his sources—he made them up!" she cried. "Don't let his lies destroy your soul, as well."

"With the flick of a pen, that man took away my livelihood and the professional respect I had spent a lifetime cultivating. It doesn't matter if we win or lose—the damage has already been done." Devon shuddered, and Lana thought he might burst into tears. He kissed his wife tenderly on the forehead. "I need some air. I'll meet you outside. Don't rush on my account."

Evelyn's lip trembled as her husband walked away.

When the O'Tooles shuffled to the front of the display case, Paddy mumbled, "That's it? We waited in line to see two pages?"

"The Book of Kells is one of medieval Europe's greatest treasures. It is certainly the most famous medieval illuminated manuscript, and one of the oldest. You should be grateful they are able to display any of its pages to the public," Evelyn stated without looking up, as if she was used to having convince others of why they should appreciate historical objects.

The security guard cleared his throat and nodded towards the exit, prompting the group to head upstairs. The deliciously musty smell of old paper wafted towards them as the doors to the Long Hall opened. The sight before her took Lana's breath away.

"Was Harry Potter filmed here? It looks just like something out of Hogwarts!" Kitty exclaimed.

"I don't think so, but I wouldn't be surprised if it inspired J.K. Rowling's vision," Lana agreed.

It was truly magical being inside such a massive library, literally surrounded by walls of books. A small sign stated that two hundred thousand of the library's oldest tomes were housed here in the oak shelves. Every few feet there was a bookcase filled with hundreds of books, so tall a ladder was needed to reach those at the top. Connecting the two facing shelves was a curved roof of carved wood. Gorgeous cast-iron circular staircases wound up between the two floors.

Their group walked along the center of the Long Hall, in a corridor running the length of the rectangular space. Sculptured busts of the world's great philosophers lined the main path. Velvet green ropes cordoned off the book-filled enclaves. Several illustrated books were displayed under glass in the center of the hall, as was the Brian Boru Harp, the oldest surviving harp in Ireland and the model for the insignia of Ireland.

It was incredibly busy with tourists slowly walking along the displays, meaning it took quite a bit of time to move through the Long Hall. Lana examined the gigantic hall filled with case upon case of books. As she gazed up at the many tomes, Lana wondered how many eyes had read the billions of words printed on their collective pages.

When she noticed Evelyn standing just behind her, at the back of the group, Lana saw her chance to chat with her guest, without making the others curious. Whatever marital tensions the Rileys were experiencing, it was part of Lana's job to ensure their discontent did not negatively affect the group's dynamic.

"Hi, Evelyn. I can't help but notice that there's some tension between you and your husband. Is there anything Randy or I can do to help alleviate your stress?" Experience had taught her that it was best to be blunt when dealing with bickering or unsatisfied guests. Evelyn's eyes narrowed as she regarded her. Lana figured there was a fifty-fifty chance that her guest would blow her off or accuse her of being impertinent.

After a long silence, Evelyn said, "There is not much you can do. Our stress has nothing to do with the trip. Everything is well organized; we have no complaints. Dotty is always good to her clients." She smiled, but it didn't reach her eyes.

"Is there anything we could do to help you two work out your differences? Maybe a private tour or dinner reservations at a romantic restaurant?"

Evelyn exhaled loudly. "Don't waste your time. That's our problem right now—Devon is not interested in anything. I guess that is why I have been so overly enthusiastic about everything. I was hoping it would get him excited, too, but it's not working."

"Did he recently retire? Or is he perhaps working too much?" Lana pushed, truly curious as to why Devon seemed to be absent and uninterested in life. This might also be the reason for their not traveling as much with Wanderlust Tours.

Evelyn turned away from Lana and sighed. "His business went bankrupt a year ago, and he's been struggling to deal with that loss, as well as finding a new passion to replace it. He put his heart and soul into his business for thirty-five years, and losing it has been incredibly traumatic—for both of us, really. When I retired last month, I thought traveling again would help energize him again. Because we both have Irish ancestors, I thought that might trigger something in him. But it doesn't seem to be doing the trick. It's as if the light burning inside of him has been extinguished and there is nothing I can do to relight it."

Lana squeezed Evelyn's shoulder lightly. "It's early days. Maybe he just needs more time to relax and unwind. The first few days of this tour are really busy, I know, but we have built quite a bit of free time into the last four days of our trip. If there's anything you two want to do, let me know and I'll set it up for you."

"Thank you. I'll probably take you up on your offer, once we've had a chance to review the list of optional excursions."

Lana nodded, scanning her brain for ideas that might interest them both. "Did you want to visit your ancestral homes while you're here? I know Paddy and his family are going to visit his later in the week. Where do your families hail from?"

"I'm not entirely certain. I know my grandparents both emigrated from Ireland, but I haven't really gotten started with my side yet. Devon's mother began researching their family's lineage last year, and she traced Devon's great-grandfather back to Cork County, but we don't know which town. His mom has already spent a fortune on genealogy research, and now that I'm retired, I thought I could take it over for her and save her some money. That's partly why we're here. I have already been in contact with the Glasnevin Cemetery's genealogy department and hope they can find something that would give us a new lead. If we are lucky, we can visit Devon's ancestral home before we fly back to the States."

"That would be incredible! I hope it works out for you both," Lana smiled, then asked, "Say, what did you do at the art museum?"

"I was a curator of decorative arts. My specialty was jewelry and tapestries—"

"Did I hear you say that you're here to trace your Irish roots?" Jeanie was suddenly at Evelyn's elbow and shoving a business card in her hand. "It is really important to go back as far as you can in your family's history if you want to discover your true lineage. I've run into a dead end with my ancestral search, as well, which is why I want to visit two parish churches and the Glasnevin Cemetery to check their records for new leads. If you need help navigating any archive while we are here, just give me a shout."

Evelyn stared at the business card in her hand, a deep frown on her face. "Actually, you already did. Last year you helped my mother-in-law, Cindy Riley, trace her family's roots back to Ireland."

"You're Cindy Riley's daughter-in-law?" Jeanie squealed. "I can't believe it! Why didn't you email me to let me know you were coming over?"

Evelyn looked at Jeanie as if she was crazy, but her reaction was gracious. "I didn't know you were flying over, either. Besides, it was a last-minute decision. When Dotty told us about this trip, I…"

"You jumped right on it, didn't you?" Jeanie rolled over her, her voice booming for all to hear. "I did the same." Jeanie threw an arm over Evelyn's shoulder. "Let me know if you want my help this week."

Evelyn gracefully untangled herself from Jeanie's embrace. "Thanks, but I am already in contact with one of the cemetery's archivists. The information you had found was pretty sparse, but I am hoping it is enough for her to find a new lead, perhaps further back in their records."

"Good for you," Jeanie said, though without heart. She turned on her heel to walk away, when she suddenly spun back around. "Say, would you be willing to write a review of Ancestors Across the Sea? Internet reviews are so crucial these days. All I would need are a couple of sentences about how I helped your mother-in-law trace her roots back to the old country. I can send you a few examples you can cut and paste from, or you can write up your own thoughts. Whatever is easier for you."

"I guess I could do that. I have read through all of the records you had found for her," Evelyn said, but her eyes made clear that she felt pressured to do so. "I will let you know once I've written something."

"Okay. I'll hold you to it." Jeanie wagged her finger at the older woman before sauntering away.

7

Miss Me?

The restaurant Dotty booked them into for dinner was one of the quaintest Lana had ever seen. Her grandmother would have approved of the mahogany paneling, lace-covered lamps, and flowery stained-glass windows. She could imagine the interior had not been updated in several decades, even though it was squeaky clean.

The waiters showed her group to five tables situated close together at the back of the narrow restaurant. Dotty had mentioned it was known for a dish called coddle. The chunks of sausage, bacon, potatoes, and onion slow cooked in a rich broth sounded like the perfect comfort food for this wintery day.

After everyone had taken their seats and the waiters had brought the first round of drinks, Lana leaned over to Randy. "We should probably check in with the guests and see if they want to book any more excursions. I bet things are going to fill up fast, especially the closer we get to Saint Paddy's Day."

"That sounds like a great plan." Randy sprung up and headed over to Devon and Evelyn. Lana took this chance to discover how she knew Nina.

"Hi, everyone. How are you doing?" she asked the O'Tooles.

"We are doing fine, thanks, Lana. Isn't this a cute café?" Nina replied.

"Did you see any other excursions you want to book for this week? I know you already have plans to go to your ancestral home on March 15."

Nina looked to her husband. "I don't think so. We both want to see some live music while we're here, but it doesn't appear to be a problem in this town." She nodded to a small podium built at the back, upon which a young singer and guitarist were unpacking their equipment. Every pub they had passed seemed to have a space for live musicians to play, and they had heard a plethora of talented buskers during their walks through the city center. It was wonderful.

"Excellent. Okay, I'll let you enjoy your drinks."

"Cheers to that," Patrick mumbled and toasted the air.

Lana knew the conversation was over, but she had to sate her curiosity before moving on to her next guests. "Nina, I apologize for asking, but I feel like we've met before, yet I cannot place your face. Were you a guest on one of my previous tours?"

Nina blushed as her husband wrapped an arm around his wife's shoulders. "Have you heard of Bleach?" he asked. "Nina played bass in the band."

Lana's eyes widened in recognition. Bleach was one of most successful bands ever to hail from Seattle. It had also been one of her favorite groups when she was a teenager, but she hadn't listened to them in ages. Their grunge music was more attuned to her teenage angst than her midlife blues. "I love your music. Bleach got me through so many rough times when I was a kid. It is an honor to meet you. I feel terrible for not recognizing you sooner."

Nina broke into a wide grin. "Sweetie, it's more than alright. I am flattered to hear you know our music and that it helped you through tough times. The band split up fifteen years ago, so it's no skin off my nose that you didn't recognize me. Besides, my hair is no longer bright green, and I prefer silk to flannel these days. Only the tattoos are the same."

"Are you still making music?"

Nina shook her head. "After the band broke up, Paddy and I got married and were blessed with five beautiful girls. I didn't want to be on the road anymore, so I started a rock club in Seattle and now I own three."

Lana grinned. "That's incredible! I don't get to go out much in Seattle anymore, but I do love to see live music. May I ask which club is yours?"

"The Alligator Club on the waterfront was my first. We opened two more locations in Ballard and Pike Place Market last year."

"Are you kidding me? The Alligator Club is my favorite place to go out! I love the funky atmosphere and phenomenal bands. Those sheep lamps are incredible," Lana gushed with sincerity. She truly did love to go there, for both the fantastic mixed drinks and funky interior, as well as the music. "Are you two the co-owners?"

"No, the clubs are mine," Nina said, "Paddy is my personal financial advisor and has definitely helped me keep all three clubs profitable, which is quite a feat." She laid a hand on her husband's chest. "He was the band's accountant."

Lana chuckled. *So that's how these two opposites met.* "Do you work for an accounting firm, Paddy? Or does Nina keep you too busy for other clients?"

"These days, she is my only client. Trust me, keeping those bars afloat is a full-time job," Paddy smiled and kissed his wife's hair. "But my firm does handle other accounts."

Mitch approached their table. "Hey, sorry to butt in, but did I hear you say you were part of Bleach?"

Nina smiled up at him. "Yeah, I was the bassist. My parents wanted me to be a singer, which is why they named me after Nina Simone, but I don't have the voice for it."

"I know what you mean," Mitch replied. "I tried singing lead vocals for my old folk band, but my voice wasn't right for our music."

"Are you still playing?" Nina asked. Her tone was polite enough, but she appeared to be a bit wary and less open than she had been a few moments ago. Lana could imagine that, as the owner of three popular and successful music clubs, she was constantly being asked to listen to a recording or to book a band she had never heard of. And during a vacation was definitely not the right time to hit her up for a booking date.

Mitch nodded enthusiastically. "I am now. We disbanded after our label went under last year, and it took a while to find my way again."

Nina clicked her tongue. "It is a tough market. Who were you with?"

"LowDown Records."

Nina cringed. "Oh, man. I heard about that fiasco. I'm sorry to hear you were affected."

"It took me a while to accept, but ultimately I'm happy it worked out this way. I've got more creative freedom and earn a lot more per sale now. And streaming services are starting to actually pay us decent money for our music. I think they are the future, to be honest."

"Good for you. I don't have the energy for it anymore, but I know my bookers are finding lots of great new bands online these days." Nina took a long sip of her drink and shifted her gaze away, past Mitch.

To Lana it was clear that she was ending this conversation, but Mitch didn't seem to notice. He remained standing, bouncing slightly on his heels as if to remind Nina that he was still there.

"Which label are you with now?" Nina asked. From her casual tone, it sounded like she really didn't care but was being polite.

"I set up my own, Anders Music. And last month, I released my first solo album as the Anders Band."

Nina's indifference melted as she clicked her fingers together. "Wait a second, you were half of Sampson & Anders—that's why you look so familiar!" She leaned over the table to get her father-in-law's attention. "Hey, Pops, Mitch is the guitar in Sampson & Anders. And now he's a singer for the Anders Band."

"To be honest, I am the Anders Band. I mean, I record all of the instruments in my home studio, but when I go on tour, I'll hire a band to play live with me."

Nina turned back to Mitch. "I apologize for not recognizing you earlier. Pops gave me a copy of your last Sampson & Anders album a few weeks ago. It's got a great folky vibe but is still danceable. That's important if you want to make money touring these days."

Patrick squinted at Mitch before a smile broke over his face. "By golly, you are Mitch Anders." He stuck his hand out. "Your music reminds me of the songs my dad loved to sing when I was young. It brings my childhood right back. I want to thank you for that."

Mitch leaned over Paddy and Nina to take Patrick's hand and shake it firmly. "Thanks, Patrick. That is a real compliment."

When Mitch turned to walk away, he noticed Lana listening in. "Most of my sales are online, but I still do have CDs printed. Here's a copy of my latest release."

He fished one out of his bag and handed it to Lana. She understood immediately why neither Nina or Patrick Senior recognized him; his photo had been so heavily airbrushed, he appeared twenty years younger than he truly was.

She smiled at her guest. "Thank you, that's really kind. I look forward to listening to it."

Nina seemed to be watching their interaction, waiting for Mitch to lay one on her, as well. When he did not, she said, "Say, Mitch, I'd like to take a listen to your new release, too, and if it is what I like to book, I'll bring you in contact with my booking agents. I don't keep track of the agenda these days, and I can't promise they have space anytime soon. But if Pops is a fan, you're worth taking a chance on."

Mitch put a hand on his heart. "What an honor. Let me give you a CD and my business card." Before Mitch could pull them out of his bag, a male voice yelled over at her group.

"It is you!"

Lana and the rest turned toward the voice. A pudgy, balding man was rushing towards Jeremy and Kitty. "I was certain my eyes were deceiving me this afternoon. I thought, 'There's no way he would dare come to Dublin.' Yet, here you are," the stranger growled.

Jeremy's drink slipped out of his hand and crashed to the ground, spraying beer and shards of glass across the floor.

"Did you miss me so much you decided to come for a visit?"

Jeremy rose to face the man, standing far above the stranger's short stature. "No one would miss you. What rock did you crawl out from under?"

"Guy!" Jeanie cried out as she rushed towards the stranger.

Lana's eyebrows shot up. Was this the same man Jeremy was so worried about running into?

When Jeanie tried to throw her arms around his neck, Guy stepped out of her embrace and sneered at her. "You are the last person I want to see."

Crushed and dejected, Jeanie slunk away. Lana was turning to go after her when she noticed several other members of her tour were also disturbed by Guy's presence. Devon was frozen in place, an expression of pure terror etched on his face. Evelyn was trying to distract him, to no avail. Mitch's eyes narrowed as he watched the stranger warily. Only the O'Tooles didn't seem bothered by Guy's presence.

Lana held her breath as she waited for clarity. When no one spoke up, Lana stepped towards the overweight stranger, smelling the strong scent of alcohol on his breath as she did. "Excuse me, who are you?"

He turned to her and held out a sweaty hand. "Guy Smith, senior reporter for the *Dublin Chronicle*."

Jeremy snorted. "Are you kidding me? Who would be stupid enough to give you a job, after all the lies you spread back in the States?"

"Says you." Guy turned to Kitty. "This must be your lovely wife. I've been reading quite a bit about you lately. It's good to put a face to the name."

Kitty paled and looked up to Jeremy in confusion. "Why would you be reading up on me?"

"You're the star in my next investigative piece about EuroBeer's acquisition of Firehouse Brewery."

"What are you talking about? I have nothing to do with that. And it's a merger, not an acquisition," Kitty replied.

Jeremy stepped in front of her and scowled down at the reporter. "I don't know what you are up to now, but whatever it is, you better leave my wife out of it."

"You're not my boss anymore. I don't have to listen to you." Guy turned towards the door and called out over his shoulder, "Check out next week's paper, Jeremy, and you'll see exactly what I mean. Ta for now."

Devon gazed down at the floor while Evelyn rubbed his back. "We can't get away from him. I am never going to be free, not as long as he's alive," Lana heard him say.

Out of the corner of her eye, she saw Mitch order a shot of whiskey and down it in one gulp.

"We shouldn't have come to Dublin," Kitty said to Jeremy, who was staring out at the street.

Feeling confused and out of the loop, Lana stood before her group. "I don't know who that person is or why you are all so upset, but please know that Randy and I will do everything we can to keep him away from you."

"You can't protect us from him," Devon said. "That man is pure evil." He rose and downed the last of his beer. "I need to take a walk and clear my head."

Evelyn took his hand. "I'm coming with you."

Devon started to untangle her fingers from his. "I need some time alone."

"No!" she screamed. "I'm not going to lose you. We can get through this, together."

Devon lay his forehead against hers. "How, Ev? We took this vacation to forget about him, and he shows up on the first full day of our tour! There is no escaping Guy."

"Remember what the counselor taught you—look for the positive. There is always a reason to live." She said it so softly, Lana wasn't entirely certain that she'd heard her correctly.

Lana stepped back to let her guests pass, unsure of what to do. Was Devon feeling suicidal, or was she imagining things? As much as she wanted to try to help him, Lana didn't feel as if it was her place. She didn't know the reason for Devon's despair. Yet, she couldn't let him simply walk away. Lana began to follow them, but as they turned to the door, Evelyn laid her head on Devon's shoulder and he wrapped an arm around her. One glance at how tightly Evelyn was holding onto his hand reassured Lana that Devon would not be alone tonight.

"The audacity. That man should be put down, like a lame horse."

Jeanie's announcement pulled Lana back to the rest of the group.

"How do you know him, Jeanie? Is he the former lover you were hoping to rekindle a romance with?" she asked.

"He is certainly not!" Jeanie responded in the haughtiest of tones. "I recognize his name from the newspapers. He ruined many a business and career, as I recall, and usually out of spite or jealousy."

Lana did not believe a word she said, but now was not the time to put her on the spot. Instead, she turned to Jeremy. "Did he used to work for you?"

Jeremy, however, was lost in his own thoughts. "What? Oh, sorry, Lana. Yes, he did write one piece for me, as a freelancer. But what is he doing working for the *Dublin Chronicle*? Why would they hire him?"

Kitty shook her head. "And why would he target me? The only newsworthy thing going on at my work right now is the merger, but I'm not involved with that, not even indirectly."

Jeremy slowly shook his head. "I don't understand either. I'm going to get in touch with my staff and have them try to find out for us. Knowing Guy, he is not even writing about you, but said those things to get under our skin—and it worked. His performance was just like his fake stories—all bluster and lies."

Kitty's frown didn't lessen. "Maybe you are right. But if he was lying, how did he know my name or who I worked for?"

Jeremy's lips pursed together. "That is an excellent question."

8

John Doe Investigates

After dinner, Lana and Randy escorted their group back to the hotel. The food was probably delicious, but her mind was so distracted by Guy's presence that she barely tasted the meal.

On the walk back, Lana sprinted to catch up to Jeremy and Kitty. They were walking close, their heads bowed together, as they whispered back and forth. When she approached, they grew quiet.

"I don't want to interrupt your vacation, but could we talk for a few minutes? That guy really struck a nerve with several guests, and it would be good to know who he is."

Jeremy looked to Kitty, who nodded slightly.

"Okay," he said, "but I'd rather we do it somewhere private."

"No problem. Let me get everyone settled for the night, then I'll treat you two to a pint at the pub across the street."

Her friends nodded tersely and took two seats in the hotel lobby, far away from the rest, while they waited for Lana to do her job.

She and Randy quickly surveyed their group and discovered that only Mitch and Patrick Senior wanted to go to a pub. The rest were too jet-lagged and preferred to stay in for the night. Lana didn't blame them. It had been an action-packed first day, and Guy's sudden appearance at the end of it seemed to have upset several of her guests, not just Jeremy and Kitty.

"Are you sure you want to get saddled with Pops? He can be a handful after

DEATH BY LEPRECHAUN

a few pints," Nina asked.

"Nina's right. Don't feel pressured to take care of the old man. He's got our numbers in his phone," Paddy added.

Patrick Senior scowled at his daughter-in-law and son, but Mitch kept nodding. "I'm happy to escort him to the pub. The Hairy Lemon is supposed to have some of the best live music in Dublin, and I'm certain the beers will be up to snuff, as well. Let me grab my guitar and we'll be on our way."

When Mitch skipped upstairs, Patrick Senior plopped down into a cushy couch, making it clear that he was not going to head up to his room, as his son and daughter-in-law hoped he would.

"I don't know if this is such a good idea," Paddy said. "It's been a busy first day, and we have six more to get through. Don't you think it would be better to catch up on your sleep tonight? It will probably help you recover from your jet lag faster."

"A locally brewed beer would do the trick better than a nap. Besides, I'm not a kid! I can decide for myself what I want to do. If I want to stay up and have a Guinness, then by golly, I'm going to do so. You two can go sleep your life away, but I'm going out to a pub with my new friend, Mitch."

Jeanie was hanging back from the rest—her thoughts not really with the group, it seemed—until she sat down on the couch next to Patrick and swung her hips into his. "You know, I think a pint would do me good, too."

Patrick scooted further down the couch. "It's a free world. I can't stop you."

Jeanie sniffed. "Wow, thanks. That's an offer a girl can't refuse. What is it with you men, anyway?" She stormed upstairs before Patrick could respond.

"What's with her?" he muttered.

Lana's eyes narrowed as she bit her tongue, in order to hold back her snarky response. If Guy was indeed the man Jeanie had flown over to visit, their reunion obviously did not go as she had hoped it would. And Patrick wasn't exactly being very gentlemanly. *Poor Jeanie*, she thought. Maybe she and Mitch would hit it off well enough that a romance could blossom. Stranger things had happened. "So Patrick, it sounds like you and Mitch are set for the night," she said instead, then pulled Randy aside.

"I would really like to talk to Jeremy and Kitty about this Guy situation. Is it alright with you if I go off-grid for an hour or two?"

"Of course. Why not take the night off? I'll let the guests know to call me if they need anything. All I was planning on doing was soaking in the tub and calling Gloria."

Lana squeezed her fellow guide's arm. "Thanks, Randy. Send her my love."

She walked over to Jeremy and Kitty. "I'm all set. Should we head across the street?"

Her friends nodded and rose, the sour expressions on their faces making it clear that neither were relishing the prospect of this conversation. They ducked into the first bar they passed right as the clouds opened up and peppered the streets with drops of rain.

After they ordered pints of cider and found a table, Lana turned to her friends. "Okay, tell me everything. Who the heck is that guy?"

"He used to be one of the most sought-after investigative journalists working on the West Coast," Jeremy began.

"Until Jeremy caught him lying about his sources and exposed him as a fraud," Kitty finished.

"What? I know I haven't worked as a reporter in over ten years, but I do try to stay informed, and I have never heard of Guy Smith. How is that possible?"

"Because he used a pseudonym to protect his identity. It was useful, considering the kinds of investigative pieces he was known for. He wrote under the name John Doe Investigates," Jeremy said, watching her closely as he spoke.

Lana rolled her eyes in recognition. "Oh, no. I remember that story! He was a freelance reporter who worked for several important magazines and newspapers. There were several exposés a few months ago about how several controversial articles he had written were actually based on fictitious sources and falsified documents. He destroyed several companies and careers with his writings, didn't he?"

"Exactly," Jeremy said, practically spitting the word out. "Two of his victims even took their own lives; they couldn't bear to live with the lies he had written about them."

Lana felt a surge of anger and sadness. "That is horrible! How could he get away with his false reporting for so long?"

"Guy's stories generated lots of interest and sold lots of copies…"

"Which translated into lots of advertising money," Kitty interjected.

"Editors were lining up to work with him, and no one wanted to believe that what he wrote was not true. It wasn't entirely their fault—Guy did falsify documents and create fake paper trails to back up the more controversial claims he made in his articles. Yet anytime a fellow reporter accused him of bending the truth, their assertions were chalked up as jealousy. There were even a few court cases brought against him, but they didn't seem to have an effect on his reputation. It took years to uncover his lies and deceit. And because his articles were always based on a kernel of the truth, it made it even more difficult for the victim to block the article's publication or deny the untrue parts of it."

"Or even want to," Kitty added. "In some cases, it might have been better for the person's reputation to let sleeping dogs lie. If they had taken him to court or accused him of defamation, Guy's lies would have been rehashed in the media, long after the original articles' publication."

"But how is it that you figured out he was lying, when no one else did?" Lana asked.

"In the article he wrote for my newspaper, he quoted a source I had put him in contact with, but the details just didn't ring true."

"What do you mean?" Lana asked.

"I had a lead on a story about a company that was laying off older employees so they would not have to pay out their full retirement benefits, but I didn't have a reporter who was skilled enough to work out the details and write it up. I knew of John Doe from his reputation, and another editor put me in touch with him. Because I had been working with that source for weeks, I had seen many of the confidential documents I figured Guy would cite in his article."

"Then my mother got sick and I took a week off to help her recover from her surgery," Kitty said. "Because I couldn't find a babysitter for the entire week, Jeremy stayed home with the kids."

"The article was published the day before I went back to work. But the piece was completely different than what I had expected. The article made it appear as if the company had also been embezzling from its workers' pension funds, but my whistleblower would not have been privy to those kinds of confidential financial records. He worked in human resources."

"That is odd," Lana murmured.

"When I contacted my source, he denied having told Guy the information published in the article, but he couldn't publicly contradict it without his boss finding out he was the whistleblower. He only agreed to talk to us because of the condition of anonymity. If his boss had found out that he had talked to the press, he would have certainly been fired on the spot."

Lana shook her head. "What possessed Guy to do it, do you think?"

"I think he was a really talented reporter who did have a knack for getting sources to open up to him. But at some point, he couldn't work his magic, so he made things up," Jeremy said.

Lana sat back and sipped on her drink, absorbing all that Jeremy had shared with her. "Okay, I get why he's mad at you, but why didn't I know that you were the one who exposed him? We've known each other for more than a decade, and this was a big scoop to keep from me."

Jeremy put his hand over hers and smiled gently. "That was intentional. I didn't know how editors or other reporters were going to react. Guy had written controversial articles for some of the most respected newspapers and magazines in the nation. To make things worse, I couldn't publicly contradict the article Guy wrote for my paper without exposing my whistleblower. In the end, I discreetly tipped off a few editors who had worked with Guy and let them know that he had intentionally falsified information in a story run in our newspaper."

"Oh, my! I can imagine that was a difficult conversation. How did they react?"

"I have to tell you, Lana, I was not certain which way they were going to go. One did try to discredit me, in an attempt to bury the truth and save his newspaper's reputation. Luckily, two did have their reporters triple-check all of Guy's sources and documents. By golly, if those articles didn't include falsified information, as well. After that, word spread, and most newspapers put distance between themselves and Guy's work."

"What a relief! But how did Guy find out that you were the person who initially exposed him to the rest?"

"That was my fault," Jeremy said. "After I talked to my whistleblower, I was so astounded by what I had learned that I immediately confronted Guy and blurted out what I knew. He knew my source only agreed to share information with my newspaper on the condition of anonymity, so Guy figured it was safe to tell me the truth. He didn't expect me to get in touch with my colleagues at other newspapers. However, after other editors began contacting him for official statements about their findings, he rightly assumed that I was the one who had tipped them off."

"Alright, I now understand why Guy is upset with you, Jeremy, and why he would want to target your wife in order to hurt you." Lana turned to Kitty. "What could you have done to be featured in one of his articles?"

"I have no idea. I don't have anything to do with the merger—I work in the marketing department as an assistant, not a manager."

"Could Guy spin it so that it appeared you were involved in the deal?" Jeremy mused aloud.

Kitty's forehead creased. "I suppose, but why? It's a fairly straightforward business deal—at least, as far as I know. I don't understand why he would be writing about the merger at all. There's nothing newsworthy about it."

Lana closed her eyes, dreading having to ask the next question. "Do you two want to stay on the tour, or would you rather go home, now that you know Guy is here?"

Kitty and Jeremy both startled at her question. "Stay, of course. Guy or not, we haven't been on vacation in eight years," he said. "I am not going to let that man ruin this week for us."

Lana held up her pint. "Glad to hear it. Cheers."

9

Breakfast Fit for a King

March 13—Day Two of the Wanderlust Tour in Dublin, Ireland

"Eat breakfast like a king, lunch like a prince, and dinner like a pauper." Lana read the sign hanging above the breakfast buffet aloud before grabbing a plate. The Irish didn't mess around when it came to the first meal of the day. Tradition stated she add bacon, sausages, egg, tomatoes, mushrooms, potatoes, and brown bread to her plate. But her stomach protested, and she veered off for the yogurt and fruit section instead. Breakfast may be the biggest meal for the Irish, but she preferred a light snack now and a large lunch later, once her body was awake and running at full steam.

Paddy, Patrick, and Nina were already seated at the back of the large hall and tucking into their meal. All three had chosen a real Irish breakfast, she noted. Patrick, however, was momentarily ignoring his food in favor of a frothy glass of Guinness. Simply thinking of drinking alcohol right now gave Lana heartburn.

Jeanie, Devon, and Evelyn sat at a table next to them, but had not yet eaten. Instead, the two women were poring over a file folder of paperwork while Devon stared off into the distance. Lana was glad to see that he and Evelyn were joining them today. After last night's drama with Guy, she wasn't certain they would want to stay in Dublin.

Devon didn't look up when Lana approached, but his wife did make eye contact and smile. Evelyn was clearly doing her best to be social and chipper, but Lana could see that she'd been crying, despite the extensive makeup she had lathered on.

"Good morning, I hope everyone slept well," Lana said as she approached. She glanced at the paperwork and saw that the pages were filled with names and dates.

"Thanks for asking, Lana. I slept like a queen," Jeanie said. "Evelyn is sharing the information her mother-in-law had already gathered about her family. Most of it is my work, but it was several months ago, and I simply don't recall everything that I'd found for her. I was hoping to help her find out more during our trip—free of charge."

Evelyn threw her hand in front of her mouth and mumbled to her husband, "Good thing. Your mom already paid her a grand for her services."

Lana's eyes about bulged out of her sockets. How could genealogical research cost so much?

Jeanie continued poring over the long lists of names and dates, apparently unaware of Evelyn's remark. "It seems pretty complete, at least until 1861. Then things get a bit fuzzy. I guess I did my job well," she laughed. "We are still missing a few key names on the Irish side. As I recall, your mother-in-law wanted to take a break from the research, to let it all sink in. I never did hear from her again."

"Because I am taking over for her. To be honest, it was getting pretty pricey."

"Discovering where you came from is priceless, don't you think?"

"That may be. But now that I am retired, I have time to help her," Evelyn rushed to add. "As you can see, Devon's great-great-grandfather owned a plot of land in Cork County, but it's not clear in which village. If we can figure that out, we can check the parish archives for more information. I'm hoping the archivist at Glasnevin Cemetery will be able to help me find out more."

"Gosh, they are good, but not all of their records are digitalized yet," Jeanie said, as if she wanted to temper Evelyn's expectations. "Did you send them this information when you contacted them?"

"Yes, I did."

"Excellent. Hopefully they will use their time to search through their oldest archives." Jeanie pulled out her telephone. "May I take a photo of your paperwork? I can take a peek in a few online archives that I have subscriptions to and see if they can help get you a step further."

"That would be great, thank you," Evelyn said. "We will have to buy you dinner later, as a token of our appreciation. Won't we, Devon?" Evelyn nudged her husband's arm with her elbow.

"Yes, that is a great idea. My mother will be thrilled to learn anything more. She has become quite obsessed with tracing our roots."

Jeanie straightened up and tossed her hair. "How kind of you. It would be an honor to dine with you both."

Lana noticed the doors to the breakfast room opening, and Mitch entering. He made a beeline towards the O'Tooles' table.

"Hi, Patrick. Are you feeling alright?"

The older man shrugged and took a sip of his beer.

"Again, I apologize for not keeping a better eye on him," Mitch mumbled to Nina, who waved off his words with a shrug.

"I only had two pints," Patrick protested.

"This big," Mitch whispered, holding his hands about a foot apart.

"I'm eighty-two years old, for goodness' sake! Let me be," Patrick snarled at Nina and Mitch.

"Good morning, everyone." Lana called out in a cheery voice, hoping to drown out the O'Tooles' disagreement. "I want to remind you all that our first tour starts in thirty minutes. It's going to be another busy, but fun, day!"

"Where are we going to today?" Patrick asked.

"On our agenda are guided tours of Grafton Street and Christ Church Cathedral, a traditional Irish stew for lunch, followed by a bus tour or shopping excursion, and finally, a tour of the National Leprechaun Museum."

"Great—more old buildings and history lessons. I better have another Guinness before we hit the road," Patrick grumbled.

"I'll join you, Dad," Paddy said and rose to order two beers.

"Isn't it a little early?" Nina murmured, but the O'Toole men ignored her.

"I'm glad to know we have time to shop today. Devon's suitcase still has not shown up. We better buy you something green before Saint Patrick's Day," Evelyn said.

"That's a good point. We don't want Devon to get pinched all day, do we?" Kitty laughed.

"Did you say National Leprechaun Museum? Are there other museums dedicated to leprechauns? And do the Irish really believe in them?" Jeanie asked.

Lana chuckled. "Not that I'm aware of. But we can ask our guide when we are there."

10

Luck of the Irish

Lana checked her watch again, wondering what was keeping Randy. After a long morning of tours and a hearty lunch, they had sent their guests off on their bus or shopping excursions, before heading back up to their respective rooms to enjoy a short break from their guide duties.

After a lengthy conversation with her boyfriend and a luxuriously long bath, Lana had been completely relaxed when she returned to the hotel lobby ten minutes earlier. However, her fellow guide's absence was bringing the stress back to the forefront.

"Who are we waiting for?" Jeanie asked. "You promised us a snack before the leprechaun museum, and I'm hungry."

"And I'm thirsty," Patrick slurred.

"I think you've had enough alcohol for today, Pops," Nina chastised.

Patrick simply rolled his eyes at his daughter-in-law.

"Where is he?" Lana growled to her watch as she tried to think up a plausible reason to hang around the lobby just a little bit longer. She picked up her phone to message Randy again when Evelyn's giggles drew her attention.

The retired art curator held her hand out in front of her face and turned it in the light as she whispered to her husband. Since they had returned from their shopping trip, both of them seemed to be in much better spirits. Curious, Lana looked more closely and realized she was wearing a thick gold band with a Celtic design engraved into it.

"What a beautiful ring!" Lana said and nodded to Evelyn's hand.

The older lady blushed and held it out for Lana to better see. "Thank you. I bought us matching Celtic rings the year we got engaged, but they were stolen during a burglary two years ago. I haven't been able to find the same design since. I thought that since we are in the old country, I might have better luck here. And sure enough, we found these in the second shop we went into!"

Devon held out his hand, as well. "And luckily for us, they had two of them in stock."

Lana noticed a sparkle in his eyes that wasn't there previously. "That's wonderful!" she enthused, glad to see that the rings had cheered him up so considerably.

Devon pulled his wife close and kissed her gently on the lips. "Yes, it is. I've got my lucky charm back."

"Oh, hon, your luck was never gone."

Devon nodded. "You're right. You've always been by my side," he said, getting an adoring smile in response.

"Mr. Devon Riley?" one of the hotel receptionists approached her group, looking to her guest for confirmation as she did.

"Yes?"

"Good news, sir. The airline just delivered your luggage to the hotel. It's been sent up to your room."

Evelyn threw her hands around her husband's neck. "That's the luck of the Irish, luv," she said with a silly clipped accent, getting a chortle out of her husband. It was the first time Lana had seen him laugh since the trip began.

Randy raced around the corner just as Evelyn released her husband from her embrace.

Lana blew out a sigh of relief. "Excellent, our group is now complete. We can head out to the taxi now."

Lana held the minivan door open for their guests, making a point of scooting in next to Randy.

"Where were you?" she asked, her voice laced with concern, as their taxi pulled into traffic.

He held his head low, as if he was afraid to meet Lana's eye. "I'm so sorry. Gloria and I were talking, and I lost track of the time."

Lana squeezed his arm. "It's okay; I know how hard this is for you two. Maybe you should talk to Dotty about booking you on fewer tours, at least until you get your house sorted out. Dotty did mention she had hired three new guides last week; I bet she can find someone to take your place."

Randy's head shook slightly. "But how will we pay our mortgage if I work less? I am going to ask if it's possible to work in the office more often, but I don't think she needs any more personnel right now."

"Dotty would want you to be happy. I'm sure she'll think up something." Lana had trouble keeping her voice even. She should have known that this would happen. Randy and Gloria recently married, they both loved kids, and they had just bought their first home together. She could only imagine how difficult that must be on them both with Randy being away so often. This was the time to start their life together as a couple, and here he was halfway around the world, spending his days and nights with strangers. Well, and Lana. As much as she wanted what was best for her friend, she knew it was going to be tough on her, too, if he stopped leading tours. They had worked so often together these past few months, she felt as if they were becoming a team. Although, if it was better for him and his family, she would be the first to wish him well, if he chose to quit.

Lana started to turn away when a thought crossed her brain. "Is Gloria, by any chance, pregnant?"

Randy paled so quickly that Lana was worried he might faint. "No, not that I know of! We would both like to have kids, but I want to figure out another way of earning a living before we start down that path."

11

National Leprechaun Museum

Lana stumbled around the room, disoriented by the sheer size of the table and chairs soaring far overhead. They were inside the National Leprechaun Museum, and specifically in a room designed to show visitors what the world would look like from a leprechaun's perspective. It was a trippy experience, as was the rest of the museum, and made Lana feel as if they had accidentally stepped through Alice in Wonderland's looking glass.

"This is delightful!" Jeanie squealed as she attempted to pick up a gigantic tea cup. "I feel right at home here."

"You don't say?" Their guide looked at her in puzzlement. "How much percent leprechaun are ye?"

Jeanie laughed. "I know have Irish blood running through my veins, but I don't know how much of it is leprechaun."

Their guide chuckled in response. Like most of the Irish they had met so far, he had a thick accent and a fantastically dry sense of humor. Though he was clearly speaking English, it was a variety Lana had never before encountered. Between the plethora of local expressions and that melodious accent, Lana struggled to decipher his stories. Apparently, she was the only one, for the rest were bent over in laughter most of the tour.

The guided tour was more of a song and dance show than a traditional rehearsed speech, but then the National Leprechaun Museum was like no other museum she had had ever visited. It was a space dedicated to Irish folklore and legends—much of which was shared as oral stories by their guide. His fantastic ability to spin a captivating tale made it a worthwhile stop.

After a trippy yet fun tour, they headed out through the gift shop. Her group spent as much time in the store as they did the museum proper, filling their baskets with copious amounts of T-shirts, keychains, bookmarks, and mugs.

"Gosh, Jeremy. I can't decide between these two. What do you think? Which one will the girls like better?" Lana heard Kitty say. She looked over to see Kitty holding up two garden statues in the form of a leprechaun, one leaning against a pot of gold and the other holding a small bag of coins.

Jeremy studied them critically. "How about neither?"

Lana was with him. She'd always thought leprechauns were a little scary, and their visit to the museum had not helped.

"Come on, Jeremy. You can't get much more kitschy than a garden gnome from the Leprechaun Museum," Kitty said, standing her ground.

Jeremy took hold of one of the foot-long statues, and his eyes popped open. "That thing is as heavy as my suitcase. What is it made of—lead?"

"No, the bottom half is filled with concrete. They weight them that way so they won't topple over as easily."

Jeremy stared at its face. "His smile is kind of disturbing, but his costume is pretty adorable."

Lana picked one up off the shelf, also surprised by its weight. The small statue felt as if it was made of solid concrete. Lana wondered whether Kitty was going to have to pay extra to fly it back.

"I thought the kids would love it. You know how they like to paint garden gnomes onto rocks. This is the real thing."

Jeremy squeezed his wife's shoulder. "You are right. We did promise to bring them back lots of souvenirs. They'll love this statue as much as they will love wearing their 'Kiss me, I'm Irish' T-shirts."

Kitty rolled her eyes. "You promised we wouldn't buy those…"

"If you get to buy that creepy little leprechaun, then I get to buy us all these shirts. You won't have to wear them too often," he laughed.

Kitty kissed him on the cheek. "That sounds fair to me."

12

Running Into Guy

Lana scooped her pint up off her table seconds before an Irish lass did a jig across it, laughing as she danced her way across the room. When Lana put her drink back down, a local man grabbed her hand and pulled her into a close embrace before twirling her around the pub's makeshift dance floor. Lana tried not to bump into the other tables, an almost impossible task, yet no one seemed to care. Most pints were in someone's hands, swaying in time with the lively music, just as she and her group were.

There was something so festive and happy about Irish dance music that made it impossible to sit still or be melancholy, especially once the pints started flowing. Kitty and Jeremy sashayed their way around the floor, their matching "Kiss Me I'm Irish" T-shirts reflecting in the multicolored lights. Paddy spun his wife around, then pulled her close. He moved well, especially for a tall man, and it was clear by how they looked at each other that the two were quite in love.

Evelyn and Devon were also dancing hand in hand, though theirs was more formal in style. Jeanie was standing on the sidelines, drumming one hand on her thigh. Even Patrick was getting into it, swinging his pint in between sips. Mitch was up on stage, performing with the locals, as if he was part of the band. It was quite impressive to see.

When the song ended, the pub exploded in applause. Nina and Paddy made their way over to the group's table to take a drink as the band started up the next number.

"Mitch can really play, can't he?" Lana shouted to Nina, who nodded enthusiastically in response.

"He's great! I listened to his latest release last night. It's exactly the sort of music we love to book into the Alligator Club."

"I'll have to keep an eye on your agenda—that would be a kick to see him play in one of your clubs," Lana gushed, feeling the cider's effect on her body. She normally didn't drink much during a tour, but it was almost impossible to avoid alcohol in Dublin, especially when almost all of their meals and nights out were in pubs. Besides, she had never tasted such a sweetly dry cider before and was loving the local brews. Her clients claimed the Guinness also tasted better here, but she had to take their word for it. She rarely drank beer back home.

An unplanned stop in a pub after their tour of the Leprechaun Museum meant they almost missed their dinner reservation, which left them no time to go back to the hotel and drop off their souvenirs. Randy and Lana took it upon themselves to guard everyone's bags so their clients could enjoy the evening without worrying about their stuff being stolen. They'd piled their clients' considerable number of purchases under two tables at the back of the bar and had been taking turns keeping an eye on it.

After several drinks and dances, nature called and Lana made her way along the edge of the crowded dance floor to the toilet. The hallway leading to the bathrooms was long and narrow with a plethora of old photos covering the yellowing walls. Unfortunately, two of the three lights were out, and the four doors were poorly marked.

Lana opened the first, revealing a mini-kitchen and dishwashing station, bustling with workers. After apologizing for intruding, she backed out and opened the second. The smell of urine and garbage emitting from the overflowing dumpster temporarily overwhelmed her. When she saw something scurrying towards her, Lana quickly pulled the door to the back alley closed and tentatively opened the next one. When she did, the tiny symbol of a woman crossing her legs was lit up by the bathroom's single bulb.

"Phew," she murmured, glad to have found the correct spot. After doing her business and touching up her makeup, Lana weaved her way back along the hallway. Moments before she passed the kitchen, the door flew open and a muscular dishwasher stepped out. He pushed the door to the back alley open with his elbow, threw a bucket of dirty water onto the pavement, then stepped back into the kitchen, before Lana could process what was happening.

"I think I've had too much to drink," she chastised herself aloud as she returned to her group. They were all tipsy and giggly at this point, which was not surprising considering how many pints they had consumed.

The band was taking a five-minute break, and most of the pub's patrons were using the opportunity to order another drink. Randy and Mitch were standing next to their table. When she approached, Mitch was cradling his guitar; Randy, an empty beer glass. Both men appeared to be people watching.

"What is your guitar's name?" Lana dared to ask.

Mitch laughed. "How do you know she has one?"

"I don't, but seeing how you hold onto her, I figured she might have. A friend of mine plays the trombone and calls his instrument Lucille."

"My old lady's name is Grace. She's got the style to pull it off."

Lana regarded the vintage guitar and considered the name, before nodding. "I like it. It's classy."

A gruff voice pulled Lana's attention back to the dance floor. Patrick was approaching the table fast, with Jeanie trailing close behind.

"What do you think you're doing, woman? Get your hands off my backside," Patrick admonished as he sprinted towards Lana, Randy, and Mitch. "You keep following me around like a puppy dog. Don't you get it—I'm not interested in you."

"Well, I never!" Jeanie stopped when he reached their table, then turned on her heel and scurried away.

"What was that all about?" Lana asked, hiding a smile behind her hand.

"That woman can't keep her hands off of me. But I'm not interested in a vacation romance. I just want to have a drink and listen to good music. I don't need some young hussy pushing up my blood pressure."

Lana raised an eyebrow; Jeanie was in her fifties and would probably love to be referred to as a young hussy.

A shout at the door made her whip her head around. *What is going on now?* she wondered. A group of customers, presumably locals, were entering and yelling their hellos to the bartenders. They returned the greeting, before turning back to the plethora of clients lining the bar.

"What is this, happy hour? Locals should get to cut in front of tourists, right lads? Especially during Saint Patrick's week," a familiar voice shouted above the rest.

"Acting the maggot, Guy?" a bartender yelled back, getting a chuckle out of his friends. "Did you say locals? Or imports who think they own the place?" The bartender said it with such sarcasm that most of the local patrons broke out in laughter.

Lana's face drained of color when she recognized the bartender's target. It was Guy Smith, the reporter Jeremy had exposed as a fraud! Unfortunately, the rest of her group had spotted him, as well. Both Jeanie and Evelyn stood frozen in the middle of the dance floor, glaring at Guy as if they couldn't believe their eyes. Devon was close to the podium, his mouth agape. Kitty seemed to be holding Jeremy back, but his vibe of hatred was so strong it was palpable.

Apparently, Lana wasn't the only one who could feel it. Guy turned to Jeremy, and a wave of pure rage crossed his face.

"That man is a criminal. He shouldn't be allowed in here," Guy roared as he pointed to Jeremy.

"If we kept the criminals out, we wouldn't have many customers left, would we?" another bartender joked, getting a rise out of the pub's patrons.

"Come on, Guy, why don't we go to the pub next door," said a short woman with bright pink hair as she tried to pull him to the front door.

Guy shook off her hand. "I'm not stepping aside for him. He cost me everything! Dublin is my town, and he is not welcome here." He crossed his arms over his rather large belly, practically daring Jeremy to react.

The fun and relaxed atmosphere vanished immediately. The bartenders must have sensed it, too, because they rang a bell hanging above the bar, and the band sprung back up onto the podium.

"Time for a song, eh?" the singer cried into the microphone before launching into a melancholy number that sent most patrons into their lovers' arms. The music was so loud, Guy and Jeremy's fight was drowned out. Both men quickly gave up and retreated to their respective tables, luckily on opposite sides of the pub.

Lana went to her friend, who was shaking visibly. "How are you holding up, Jeremy?"

He simply shook his head.

"I need to talk to my husband privately. We'll be right back. I promise," Kitty said before pulling her husband towards the back of the bar, close to the toilets.

Randy shook his head. "Bad luck having that guy show up here. Do you think our guests are going to want to leave?"

"That's a good question—I think we should ask them. Though no one's come back to get their coats or scarves, so I guess they aren't in any hurry."

"Good point. If we are going to stay a while longer, would you mind if I got another beer? The Guinness really does taste better here," Randy said.

"Sure. I'll watch the bags until you get back."

"Do you want another cider?"

Lana considered it, but her head was already beginning to throb a little. "Probably better not to—but thanks."

She scanned the pub for the rest of her clients as Randy joined the long line leading up to the bar. Through the thick crowd, Lana caught a glimpse of Patrick, back on a bar stool, happily sipping a lager. Paddy and Nina were up at the front of the stage, dancing to the now up-tempo song. Jeanie and Evelyn, however, were standing a few feet away from the table, both trembling with anger and staring in Guy's direction. Their conversation became increasingly heated. When Jeanie began miming that she was throttling someone, Lana figured it was more important to make certain her guests didn't do anything rash than to guard their souvenirs.

Lana pushed through the crowd to reach her clients. "How are you two holding up?" she asked as soon as she was within hearing range.

"That man destroyed my husband, so I'm not doing that great right now," Evelyn snapped, her gaze never leaving Guy. However, her target didn't seem to notice because his attention was focused on Jeremy and Kitty, still standing close to the hallway leading to the toilets, deep in conversation.

"Why couldn't he have picked another bar?" Jeanie cried. "Maybe we should leave. I don't know if I can keep my hands off his throat if we stay much longer."

That must be her former lover; otherwise why would Jeanie be so angry with Guy? Lana thought. But why did she lie about how she knew him? Was she ashamed to have dated such a vile man, or was she unwilling to accept that he had rejected her again?

"Maybe we should go to a different bar," Lana agreed. "I know Jeremy is also really upset, and there are enough pubs with live music in Dublin. Hey, where is Devon?" Lana asked, searching the dance floor for her client.

"Devon was dancing a minute ago," Evelyn said, her voice trailing off as she scanned the room.

Jeanie stalked off without responding.

Lana looked towards the podium. Devon had spent most of the evening dancing close to the tiny stage. Since he and Evelyn had found their Celtic rings again, he seemed much more energetic and interested in life. *Funny how such a little thing like that can make such a big difference, at least to those who are superstitious,* Lana thought.

But now, she didn't see Devon dancing, and Mitch was also absent from the podium. *Where did they go?* Lana looked towards their tables and noticed Mitch's guitar was propped up in one of the chairs. He must have gone to use the toilet, she figured, if he'd left his beloved instrument behind.

"I don't see him anywhere," Evelyn said, panic in her voice. "Did he go to the bathroom? I wonder if he saw Guy come inside. I need to keep Devon away from that creep. Running into Guy again might put him right back in therapy or land him in jail. I'm going to go look for him."

Lana frowned at her client. What was she talking about? How did Devon and Guy know each other?

Evelyn begun weaving her way towards the restrooms. "Let me help you," Lana said. She was following her client when a cry from the opposite side of the bar drew her attention.

"What do you think you're doing?" Guy screamed.

Lana jumped up on the nearest chair to better see what was going on. Liquid was dripping off of Guy's chin, and his shirt was soaking wet. Jeanie stood before him, a triumphant look on her face and an empty glass in her hand. "People like you should be put down. You're only good for making trouble!"

Jeanie began hitting him over the head with her handbag, bringing his small group of friends to tears of laughter. Guy held up his hands to fend off her attack, but did not try to restrain her otherwise. "Leave me alone, you crazy broad!"

"Jeanie—stop it! He's not worth it!" Lana called out as she rushed over. When she reached her client, Jeanie fell into her arms and began weeping uncontrollably. Lana rubbed her back, trying to comfort her as best she could.

Guy wiped his face off with a few napkins, but it had little effect. "I'm going to the toilet to get cleaned up," Lana heard him say to his friends. "Order me a pint, will you?"

Once Guy walked away, Jeanie's tears dried up quite quickly. Lana handed her a handkerchief anyway.

"Thank you, my dear." Unfortunately, the tears had loosened her extensive makeup and the handkerchief did more smearing than cleaning. When she handed the cloth back to Lana, Jeanie looked like a very sad clown.

"Oh, hon, your makeup got a little bit messed up. I think you better go to the bathroom and clean your face off with soap."

"I just want to leave this wretched place. Can't it wait until we get back to the hotel?"

Lana shook her head.

"Is it that bad?"

Lana nodded as Jeanie pulled out a foldup mirror. Her mouth formed a tiny O when she caught a glimpse of her reflection. "I'll be right back."

When Lana turned back towards their table, she noticed Paddy shaking Patrick's shoulder, trying to get his father's attention. The older man's head was nodding forward, and Lana suspected he was about to fall asleep.

"Can I get you a taxi back to the hotel? Or would you prefer to stay a while longer?"

"We better go now, otherwise Pops is going to sleep on the bar," Nina said.

"I'm not going anywhere!" Patrick Senior yelled and slammed his pint glass down.

Before Paddy or Nina could respond, the crash of glass and a blood-curling scream arose from the back of the bar. Seconds later, a young dishwasher tore into the bar and straight into a bartender's arms. "There's a dead man in the alley!" she cried. "Murdered by a leprechaun, he was!"

13

This Is A Crime Scene

"Did she say a leprechaun killed someone?" Lana asked aloud, but no one answered. Most patrons were too busy grabbing their things and rushing out of the bar. Lana and Randy went against the tide, pushing their way towards the back where several patrons and most of her guests were gathered around the entrance to the narrow hallway. Lana noticed the woman with the pink bob was there, too, along with the rest of Guy's group.

A skinny young man wearing a T-shirt with the pub's logo on it stood inside the doorway, blocking them from entering the space.

"The police are on their way—please return to your tables," he yelled, sending most of the crowd scurrying back to their places.

Kitty was standing behind him, farther down the hallway, yelling to her husband, whom Lana could not quite see. However, when she stood up on her toes, she spotted him through the open alley door, being held in a headlock by the dishwasher who had surprised Lana earlier. Jeremy frantically called out to Kitty. When he reached out to her, Lana noted that his palms were coated in red.

"I told you to stay back—this is a crime scene!" the muscular man holding her husband yelled at Kitty when she tried to move closer.

"Kitty!" Lana cried as she pushed her way around the skinny employee and rushed to embrace her friend.

"What happened?" Lana asked, though one look at the scene outside the alley door told her enough.

Sprawled facedown on the ground was Guy, a pool of red encircling his head. Lying next to his body was a creepy little leprechaun statue. It looked exactly like the one Kitty and Jeremy had purchased for their daughters.

Lana's stomach dropped as a moan escaped her throat. "Please don't be the same statue," she murmured.

"Lana! It's not what it looks like!" Jeremy screamed. "The door was open, and I saw Guy lying in the alleyway. I was checking for a pulse when that dishwasher saw me standing over him. I didn't do this!"

"Let my husband go! He wouldn't harm anyone!" Kitty shrieked.

"That's for the Gardai to decide. All I know is that your husband was doing a runner when I stopped him."

"That's not true! I never would have left Kitty alone," Jeremy protested. "I was going back inside to…"

"Step aside," a male voice called out from behind. Lana and Kitty turned to see a group of uniformed police officers entering the hallway, "GARDA" on their dark blue uniforms. Rain dripped off their dark blue caps, each embellished with a golden, sun-shaped medallion.

An older officer approached Lana and Kitty. "Please return to your table and wait for us to question you," he said, then stepped between them and out to the alleyway without waiting for an answer.

He approached the muscular dishwasher holding onto Jeremy and scratched at his chin. "What have you caught there, lad?"

"A killer, if I'm not mistaken," the dishwasher said, pride in his voice.

"Shall we take him off your hands?" Two uniformed officers stepped in and grabbed Jeremy's arms. When they twisted them behind his back and snapped cuffs onto his wrists, Kitty cried out, "My husband didn't murder anyone!"

"Ma'am, please return to your table."

Kitty crossed her arms over her torso. "I am not going anywhere. That is my husband, and he did not harm anyone. If you are taking him to the station, then I demand you let me ride with him."

The man started to refuse, but one look at Kitty made it clear that "no" was not an option. "Let me ask if you can ride back to the station." The officer then looked to Lana. "You should go back inside. We'll want to be interviewing everyone about what they saw and heard."

"Lana, can you call my newspaper and let them know what is happening? Hopefully they can arrange a lawyer for me, somehow," Jeremy yelled to her.

"I'll do better than that—I'll call Dotty and have her recommend a local law firm," Lana responded. "I know you wouldn't hurt anyone."

When the officers pulled Jeremy towards a police car, Kitty followed. Moments after the police car holding Jeremy pulled away, another followed with his wife in the back.

As Lana passed the open door, she looked again at the crime scene. The leprechaun's eyes seemed to be following her. She double-timed it back to the table, hoping to check Kitty's bag of souvenirs before the police questioned them.

However, when she approached the table, Evelyn rushed over to her.

"Lana, what are we supposed to do?" The retired art curator addressed her, but Evelyn's gaze was fixated on the policemen milling around the hallway. Most of her group were gathered around their table, also nervously watching the police's comings and goings. Only Patrick lay slumped over in a chair, snoring loudly.

Lana glanced around the pub and noticed that most of the patrons had already fled. Two officers were questioning the few patrons still seated at the bar, jotting down notes about the night's events. Lana noticed that the woman with pink hair was no longer inside.

Another group of police officers arrived, meaning it wouldn't take long for them to interview the remaining patrons and their group. Once they were done, Lana could call Dotty and arrange for a lawyer. Seeing as Jeremy had the motive, weapon, and opportunity, and was caught literally red-handed at the crime scene, he would need the best of the best. Dotty could afford it, and Lana would do all it took to pay her back.

"The police are going to want to question everyone. We better stay here until they are done, then we will get a taxi back to the hotel," Lana said.

Evelyn nodded in response, then took her place next to Devon. Her husband, however, did not seem distressed or anxious. Considering how strongly he had reacted to Guy's presence, Lana had expected him to be an emotional wreck. In fact, he seemed to be suppressing a smile. *What is going on with him now? And does it have anything to do with Guy's death?* she wondered.

She glanced under the table at the bags by her feet. Kitty's bag was the heaviest, so she had placed it towards the front and at the bottom of the pile. As slyly as she could, Lana knocked a coaster off the table, then made a show of bending over to pick it up. She didn't even need to open the bag; the shape alone told her enough—the bulky statue was no longer inside.

She squeezed her eyes shut, unable to accept that her friend had smashed the leprechaun over the reporter's head. "There must be another explanation," Lana muttered.

A young police officer made his way over to their table, his notepad at the ready. After a brief round of introductions, he asked, "Where were you all when the victim was discovered?"

He nodded to Jeanie, the guest closest to him, and put his pen to paper. "I was powdering my nose," she said, holding her chin up high.

The young man looked at her in puzzlement, until Lana said, "She was in the bathroom."

"Fixing my makeup," Jeanie added as she batted her eyelashes at the young man. "What do you think? Do I look stunning?"

The man blushed as he mumbled, "You're old enough to be my mum."

Jeanie jerked her head away.

"Did you know the victim…" The officer checked his notepad. "Guy Smith?"

"I most certainly did not. From what I hear, the man was a bad egg. He falsified sources to spice up his news articles. That's plagiarism, if you ask me!"

"You mean 'defamation,'" Lana said softly.

"Plagiarism, defamation, you get what I mean."

The officer scratched at his chin with his pen. "And how do you know all of this about him, seeing as you don't know him?"

"The story of his rise and fall was widely covered in the national newspapers back home. It's not as if I needed to have met him before to know what a scoundrel he was."

Lana started to open her mouth, but quickly thought better of it. She had no proof that Jeanie and Guy were once romantically involved.

The man wrote up Jeanie's statement, then looked to Patrick. "What happened to him?"

"A few too many pints, I'm afraid," Paddy said. "Dad will be fine once we get him back to the hotel where he can sleep it off."

"We arrived yesterday and haven't yet gotten used to being in a different time zone," Nina added when the young man's concerned expression didn't lessen. "My husband and I were trying to wake Pops up when we heard the screaming. He slept right through that, as well. Lana can confirm what happened—she was standing next to me, about to arrange a taxi for us, when that girl burst into the bar."

The officer looked to Lana for confirmation. "That's right. We were talking about going back to the hotel when Guy Smith's body was discovered."

He dutifully jotted down her statement, then turned back to Nina and Paddy. "Jet lag and alcohol can be a dangerous combination, especially for an older gentleman. I hope you will keep an eye on him tonight."

Nina pressed her hand to her heart. "We promise to take good care of him."

"Did you know the victim?"

"Never heard of him. But we aren't as well-read as Jeanie here," Nina said and grinned at the genealogist as Paddy nodded in agreement.

The policeman looked to Mitch, who was standing with his guitar over his shoulder, as if he might break out in song at any second. "I was up on stage when that young lady came in yelling about a murder. The band invited me to join them, and we'd been playing together most of the night. I had not heard of Guy before coming on this trip."

Lana startled at his answer. Mitch was not up on the podium when Guy's body was found. She didn't know exactly where he was at that moment, but because his guitar was at their table, she figured it was the bathroom.

The officer's eyes wandered over the guitar before he turned to Randy.

"And you, sir?"

"I was waiting in line to buy a beer. I'm with Mitch—I had never heard of Guy before coming to Ireland."

When the officer turned to Devon and Evelyn, the Rileys stiffened. "We were on our way to the bathrooms when that girl burst inside screaming. But it was so crowded, we hadn't yet made it across the dance floor," Evelyn said as she took her husband's hand. Devon nodded yet said nothing.

Lana's forehead creased. That wasn't right. Evelyn was going to check on Devon, who had rushed to the bathroom after Guy had entered the bar. Did she go to Devon after Jeanie threw the drink in Guy's face? Or before? Lana rubbed at her temple, attempting to reconstruct this chaotic evening in her mind, but the precise timing of events was lost to her. Too much had happened at the same time, and the many pints she had consumed were messing with her memories.

"And did either of you know the victim?"

Evelyn's eyes widened, and her mouth froze. Devon leaned forward to answer for both of them. "We had read about the false articles in the newspapers, but I had not met the man in person before."

The young officer nodded, then turned his attention to the large pile of bags under the table. "It seems your group had time to shop before coming to the pub."

"Yes, everyone bought souvenirs at the Leprechaun Museum. That was our last stop before we came here."

The young man's eyes began to sparkle. "I thought that fairy looked familiar."

Lana cocked her head. "What do you mean?"

"My cousin is a tour guide at the National Leprechaun Museum. He's a great storyteller and took to the job right away. His name is Conor. I wonder if he was your guide today."

"What does that have to do with anything?" Jeanie asked, her tone indignant.

The man ignored her and picked up the topmost bag. "May I take a peek inside your bags? I promise not to steal anything," the policeman said and winked.

Lana nodded yes, afraid her voice would crack if she tried to respond audibly.

"Let's see what Devon and Evelyn purchased." He opened the bag marked with their names, pulled out the purchase receipt, and made a show of comparing it to the items inside. "The contents match," he finally said.

Next, he examined the three bags marked "Jeanie," again checking the receipts against the purchases.

He continued to inspect the bags without further comment, until he reached the bottom bag, marked "Kitty and Jeremy."

Lana's heart sank as she realized what he was about to discover. Indeed, seconds after reading through the receipt and inspecting the bag, he looked to Lana and Randy.

"Seeing as these two are currently at the police station, can either of you tell me where the two adult-sized 'Kiss Me I'm Irish' T-shirts are? They were purchased today but aren't in here."

Lana almost melted in relief. "They pulled those shirts on after they got to the pub."

"Let's see what else is missing." The officer dumped the bag's contents onto their table and made a show of sifting through the shamrock key chain holders, pot-of-gold bookmarks, and kid-sized "Kiss Me I'm Irish" T-shirts. "Funny thing, that. It says here that they bought a leprechaun statue, but I don't see one."

The officer looked again to Lana and Randy. "Thing is, my cousin gave my gran a leprechaun that looks just like the one used to murder our victim. And he got it from his employer's gift shop."

The man's accent turned "thing" into "ting," and the rest of the sentence became a melody, despite the seriousness of his words.

The officer placed all the items in the bag before slipping the receipt inside his notepad. When he snapped it shut, Lana's stomach bunched up into a knot.

"I'll be taking this with me as evidence. Stay here a moment, will you?"

The officer walked over to his superior, keeping one eye on the group as if to ensure they didn't try to escape. Considering the room was full of police and two were standing guard at the door, Lana doubted they had much chance of slipping out of here unseen.

After a brief conversation, the young officer returned with his boss in tow.

"Hello, I'm Detective Inspector Sheraton. So, my sergeant tells me that Jeremy Tartal was part of your group. Are you a group of friends traveling together or is this an organized tour?"

"It's a tour organized by Wanderlust Tours, a company based out of Seattle, Washington. Randy and I are leading it," Lana responded, nodding to her fellow guide as she did.

"How long are you here for?" the detective asked, his tone jovial.

"It's a seven-day tour of Dublin and the surrounding area. We arrived yesterday."

He broke out into a grin. "Grand. That will give you plenty of time to enjoy the city before it gets busier with tourists coming in for the Saint Patrick's Day parade."

Lana smiled and nodded, hoping it covered her nervousness.

The detective looked around the table. "Are there more in your group?"

"No, it's us, plus Jeremy and Kitty. But they are on their way to the police station." Lana had trouble keeping the irritation out of her voice. "I'm certain that, once you've talked to Jeremy, you'll see that he's not a killer."

"Thanks for the tip." He winked. "Can I have a copy of your itinerary and list of passengers? Preferably one with the passport numbers noted."

"Certainly. Do you want a digital copy, or a printout?"

"I prefer paper. I like the feel of it."

Lana dug through her bag and pulled out copies of both documents.

The officer smiled as he took possession, adding, "I don't expect to be calling on you, but it's better to be prepared, don't you think?"

Why was the Irish accent so darn adorable? It made it difficult to take anything that the officers said seriously.

"Of course. But what is going to happen to Jeremy? He didn't hurt anyone; he was simply checking for a pulse," Lana pushed.

"His wife, Kitty, is also at the police station. She can keep you informed of our investigation. Enjoy your time in Dublin." He tipped his hat at her and the group before returning to the crime scene. Lana shivered when she noticed a forensics team, draped in white, stepping out into the alleyway.

Randy turned to her, his eyes wide open. "This is bad. Do you want to go to the police station, as well? I can get our group back to the hotel."

Lana was so grateful that he was so competent and capable. "I need to get back to the hotel, too, so I can call Dotty and let her know what's happening. Though I bet once the police talk to him, they'll see it was all a big misunderstanding and let him go."

"I don't know, Lana. From personal experience, I know the police aren't keen on releasing a suspect until they have another one to replace them with. At least, the Italian police were like that."

Lana put a hand on her friend's shoulder. Only three months earlier, it had been Randy in a jail cell, wrongly accused of murdering an ex-girlfriend. Through a lot of luck and eavesdropping, Lana had managed to figure out who the real killer was and get Randy released from police custody in time for his wedding.

They gathered up their group's many purchases as the rest pulled on their jackets. It was a somber ride back to the hotel, and she was spared much chit-chat about the reporter's demise. Luckily, her guests knew that she and Jeremy were friends; otherwise, she feared, the tone might have been gossipier. Right now, Lana couldn't take anyone even joking about him being a killer.

As soon as they returned and everyone was back in their hotel rooms, Lana called the owner of Wanderlust Tours.

"Lana Hansen, how are you doing, my dear?" Dotty sounded chipper and bright; Lana felt bad that she was about to spoil her boss's mood.

"Not so great, I'm afraid. There has been a situation, and the police have taken Jeremy in for questioning."

"Was someone murdered? Why do so many of our clients get killed on your tours?"

Lana blew out her cheeks. "I wish I knew so I could prevent it from happening ever again. But it wasn't a client this time, it was a reporter for a local newspaper. He and Jeremy once worked together back in the States. It's a long story, but the short of it is, the man blames Jeremy for his firing. I guess I should say 'blamed.'"

"Did Jeremy attack him? Why do the police have him in custody?"

"Jeremy found the reporter's body and was checking for a pulse when the pub's dishwasher stumbled upon them. He swears he didn't do it, but did have Guy's blood on his hands."

"That does not sound good."

Lana sprung off her bed and began pacing the room. "No, it's not. Look, I'm sorry to be abrupt, but the cops want to interrogate him, and Jeremy needs a lawyer. I hate having to ask, but could you recommend a local one for us?"

"You know I'm happy to do so, though I am sorry that it is necessary again."

Lana stared out her window, watching buskers singing on the sidewalks, couples strolling arm in arm, and lines forming at the more popular pubs. More than anything, she wished Jeremy and Kitty were out on the town, enjoying great music and a pint of lager, instead of sitting in an Irish police station. "Trust me, I wish this hadn't happened, either."

"Poor Kitty. Give her a hug for me, will you? Let me contact my lawyer and see what he says. I'll give you a call as soon as I have a name."

"Thanks, Dotty. You're a lifesaver."

14

Killers For Clients

"Darn it! Who could it be?" Lana bashed her knuckles against her temple as she tried to recall her guests' movements in the few minutes before the reporter's body was found. Guy couldn't have been dead long, Lana reckoned. Jeremy said the alley door was open and the reporter's body was clearly visible from the hallway; that was why he went out to check on him, as any normal human being would have. Which meant Jeremy must have been the first person to have walked past that door, after the killer had struck.

Who else was in the hallway at that moment? From her group, it sounded like Evelyn, Jeremy, Devon, Mitch, and Jeanie were either coming from or going to the bathroom, which meant they were all close to the alleyway when Guy was attacked.

Lana frowned as another thought struck. If the killer used a statue to murder Guy, then it was premeditated in the sense that when the murderer took it out of the bag, they did so with the intention of harming him with it.

When had the killer taken the leprechaun statue out of the bag? If only she or Randy had been at the table, keeping an eye on their clients' things, as they had agreed to do. But no, Randy had gone to the bar and she had been distracted by Jeanie throwing a drink in Guy's face. Meaning anyone in the pub could have grabbed the leprechaun and used it to murder the reporter.

Even Jeanie had the chance to do so, Lana realized. After Jeanie went off to wash her face, Lana had checked in on the O'Tooles. From the bar, she didn't have a clear view of their bags. To get to the bathroom, Jeanie would have had to walk along their table. She could have grabbed the statue on her way. And Jeanie did know that Guy was inside the men's room, drying off the drink she had thrown in his face.

But the bar was jam-packed with patrons, and through the thickness of the crowd, she couldn't have kept her eye on the hallway even if she had wanted to do so. Anyone could have killed Guy.

Her brow crinkled as she considered her last train of thought. Could anyone really have killed him? Who but their group knew that there was a heavy garden gnome under their table? No, the chance that a stranger did this was slim to none. Yet Lana was certain that Jeremy had not killed Guy, which meant that someone else in her group most likely had.

Why does this keep happening? Lana wondered. Was it simply bad luck or did she somehow attract murderers as clients? *Maybe I should start switching with other tour guides at the last minute, to see if that tempts fate and keeps the killers away*, she thought.

But for now, she had no choice but to carry on and do her best to show her clients Dublin, while keeping her ears open for any clues as to which one of them might be a killer.

Easy as pie. Unfortunately, this wasn't the first time she had been forced into this role. And she suspected it would not be the last time.

15

New Evidence

An hour later, Dotty called back with the name of an Irish law firm. One of its lawyers was already en route to the police station.

Lana thanked her boss profusely before calling Kitty to share the good news.

"Thank goodness! Jeremy really needs a lawyer now. The police want to officially arrest him."

"What do you mean?" Lana snapped. She had honestly thought the police would have realized that it was all a misunderstanding by now. "They've only had him in custody for a few hours. What reason do they have for arresting him?"

"When they interviewed Guy's fellow reporters at the *Dublin Chronicle*, they learned more about the article he was writing about Firehouse Brewery. They won't tell me what they discovered, but whatever it is, it gave the police reason to believe that Guy included me in his article in order to disgrace me, as a way of hurting Jeremy. They think Jeremy killed Guy to prevent him from finishing the article."

Lana felt her blood pressure rising. "Are you kidding me? What lies could Guy have possibly made up that would have ruined your career? We have to find out more about this article. I am going to go to his newspaper's office and see if they will share it with me."

"I appreciate your offer, but I seriously doubt that they will. Jeremy's lawyer should be able to gain access to the information, whatever it is."

"That may be, but I doubt he will be able to let you read it. Especially if the newspaper or police claim the information is confidential," Lana countered.

"But you are leading a tour—you can't walk away from your clients! Don't risk losing your job for Jeremy. Arranging a good lawyer for him is already a huge step forward."

"Jeremy has gotten me out of so many jams. And it's because of my article that he lost his job at the *Seattle Chronicle* all those years ago. I can't abandon him. Besides, Randy can cover today's tours."

"Thank you, Lana. Both Jeremy and I are grateful for your help," Kitty said, her voice trembling. "What I don't understand is why the police are so focused on Jeremy. They should be out looking for more suspects. Anyone at the pub could have killed him!"

"Technically, you are right," Lana said carefully. "But I don't see how a stranger could have done it. It must have been one of the other group members."

"Why do you think that?"

"Because of the murder weapon," she said gently, knowing Kitty's grief and anger were making it difficult for her to think clearly. "What are the odds that a stranger would have known that there was a heavy statue in one of our bags? Randy and I stashed them under that table as soon as we arrived, and no one took out their souvenirs while we were in the pub."

Kitty sighed deeply into the phone. "I guess the chances of a stranger knowing about it were slim to none. That doesn't mean that Jeremy did it!"

"You are right, he didn't do this. As far as I know, the tour will go on. I promise to keep my eyes and ears open for clues as to which one of them did this, right after I talk to Guy's colleagues."

"Do be careful, Lana. Oh, I think the lawyer just arrived. Yes, I'm over here," she called out. "I've got to go—wish us luck!"

16

A Shortage Of Suspects

March 14—Day Three of the Wanderlust Tour in Dublin, Ireland

The sudden beeping of an alarm clock startled Lana, causing her to whip over onto her stomach. Her laptop and notebook slid off her bed and tumbled to the ground. The screen lit up when it made contact with the carpet, illuminating an old photo of Devon and Evelyn Riley.

"Oopsy," she murmured as she leaned over and picked her computer and notepad.

After her second conversation with Kitty last night, Lana had fired up her computer, determined to find out all she could about Guy Smith and any possible connections to her clients. Even though all denied knowing him, whoever killed Guy must have had a reason for wanting him dead. After puzzling over several possible motives, Lana kept returning to the most logical—that one of her guests had been adversely affected by an article he had written and that, last night, they had taken their revenge.

After hours of searching through Guy's more controversial articles—the ones that received tons of publicity when they were originally published, yet were later proved to include false accusations—she had found only two connections between her guests and Guy.

The first was a vague link to Mitch that was worth exploring—if she had no other leads, that is. A story about the Seattle music label LowDown Records had caught her eye. That was the same company that had represented Mitch's band.

According to Guy's article, the label's management had embezzled millions from the musicians it represented and had moved the money through a myriad of banks into an offshore account where the funds could not be touched. To make matters worse, the label's owner had been tipped off about the article's impending publication and had skipped town before it hit the newspaper stands. Even though the owner fled the United States before he could be arrested, the label still owned the master tapes and copyrights to the published songs it had released, creating a legal nightmare for the musicians involved.

LowDown Records' demise had sent shockwaves through the Pacific Northwest's vibrant music scene. A Seattle law firm sued in the name of all of LowDown's musicians in an attempt to be compensated for their missing royalty payments, but there were too many debtors and not enough cash left in the company to pay it all back. A few famous musicians filed lawsuits to regain the rights to their music, all of which were unsuccessful. Several popular groups could not weather the financial stress and ended up disbanding. Others struggled to find a new label or were forced to create their own.

No wonder Nina had called it a fiasco. It was too bad for Mitch that he was a part of it, and that probably meant that he, too, had struggled enormously to find his way again.

Lana thought back on the article and Mitch's chat with Nina. What would the label's demise have meant for Mitch? He had said he was glad that he had finally started up his own label and had even released a new record recently. But how did he finance it all without his royalty payments?

Yet why would Mitch blame Guy for LowDown Records' demise or his financial woes? Harming the reporter would not satisfy any sense of revenge, as far as Lana could tell, and would not bring his royalty checks back.

As interesting as the connection between Mitch and the article about LowDown Records was, it was not nearly as relevant as the exposé Guy had written about six West Coast art dealers whom he accused of knowingly selling fake masterpieces to their wealthiest clients. Devon Riley's gallery, specializing in both art restoration and the sale of modern and contemporary art, was one of six firms mentioned by name in the article.

From the internet search results at her disposal, the initial piece had been reprinted in the most prestigious newspapers and magazines in the United States. Guy also penned a number of follow-up articles about specific aspects of this complex case.

The investigative piece not only caught the attention of the international media, it also prompted a criminal investigation into all six dealers and spawned several lawsuits brought on by their angry clients. From what Lana could discern from the articles, the art dealers lost almost all of the cases brought by their old clients and probably had to pay them a fortune in settlements and legal fees. The criminal investigation took months to sort out, but ultimately no charges were brought against any of the art dealers.

Soon after, the six art dealers sued Guy for defamation. Their legal team was able to prove that all six had been targeted by a professional forgery ring that had earlier been active on the East Coast. Devon had unwittingly bought four fake Andy Warhols from them—along with the accompanying paperwork—and later sold them to a local socialite. However, before selling them, Devon had the paintings examined by two different art experts specializing in Warhols. The forgeries were so good that both experts had declared all four paintings to be genuine works by the great pop artist.

Devon's lawyers had also found proof that the same forgery ring had duped several renowned art dealers on the East Coast a year earlier, with similar stories and fake contemporary paintings that passed several experts' tests. Yet, because Guy refused to share his sources with the courts, there was little the art dealers' lawyers could do to refute the claims published in his article. The courts had ruled twice, both times in favor of Guy.

Lana did a quick internet search of the art dealers mentioned in Guy's article. Of the five others besides Devon, only two were still open for business. The rest had declared bankruptcy shortly after the initial article's publication. Why had Guy intentionally ignored the facts and chosen to print these lies, instead? The fact that a forgery ring had fooled so many professionals should have been noteworthy enough.

Lana glanced again at the photo of Devon and Evelyn that she'd found online, still open on her laptop's screen. She hardly recognized the man in the picture—he seemed so full of life with Evelyn on his arm. How difficult that must have been, to lose all he had worked to build up. Yet killing Guy would not have saved his career—only getting the reporter to admit that he had lied would have done the trick.

Lana looked to her notebook. Before falling asleep, she had made a note to ask Devon and Mitch about the articles. How she would do that without offending her clients was yet to be seen. Otherwise, there were no action items listed on the page.

Before she could consider how she would approach either man, her top priority this morning was talking to any reporters currently working for the *Dublin Chronicle*. She hoped to find out more about Guy's life in Ireland, as well as get a sense of the kind of person he truly was—if any of his co-workers agreed to talk to her, that is.

A knock on the door had Lana jumping out of bed and pulling on a bathrobe in record time.

"Hi, Lana, I got your message," Randy called out through the door.

"Good morning," she said as she opened the door for her friend and fellow guide. One of her last acts before falling asleep had been to message Randy and ask him to stop by on his way to the breakfast hall.

"What's going on? You said you wanted to take the morning off." His expression was friendly enough, but his tone conveyed a layer of irritation. Lana hoped he and Gloria hadn't had another all-night conversation. He needed his sleep.

"Yeah, Kitty said they arrested Jeremy last night…"

"They what?" Randy sank onto the corner of Lana's bed. "Oh, no. He's going to need all the help he can get."

"Which is why I promised Kitty that I would check out a few things for her this morning. But I don't know how long it's going to take. Would you mind leading the morning tours? I promise to join you all for lunch."

"Of course, take all the time you need."

"Thanks, Randy. Let me get dressed and I'll see you downstairs in a jiffy."

17

A Cathartic Release

"Hi, Lana," Devon said with a smile. "Did you sleep well?" His eyes twinkled, and his voice had a playful lilt that was not there yesterday.

Not only did Devon sound different, but he looked different, too. He had switched out his loose-fitting slacks and gray sweater for a pair of purple corduroy pants and a paisley button-down shirt. Lana smiled at her guest, thrilled to see this change in attitude and clothing style.

"I did, thanks for asking. I trust you and Evelyn did, as well?"

He snuggled up to his blushing wife. "Let's just say we had a fantastic night."

Lana chuckled, glad to see her clients so upbeat. "Whatever you did, you should do it more often. You two look great." She meant what she said. Both he and Evelyn seemed to be glowing, they were so happy.

"That's a great idea," Devon said. "Although it will be hard to re-create, now that Guy is dead."

Lana froze. Was Devon freely admitting that he had murdered Guy? "What do you mean?"

He held up his hand. "This ring really is a lucky charm. It gave me the confidence and courage to face Guy, instead of running away from him, which probably saved me years of therapy."

"You what?" Lana exclaimed. "When did you talk to him?" So much had been going on that night, she had no idea that the two men had crossed paths.

"After Guy showed up, I tore off to the bathrooms to try to compose myself. That monster destroyed my life, and I refused to stick around and let him taunt me, as well. I was considering leaving via the alleyway door, but I couldn't do that to Evelyn. There I was, holed up in a bathroom stall, trembling with fright, when something snapped inside of me. I realized that I didn't want to live like that anymore. So I decided to stand up to him."

Lana's mouth dropped open. "You did?"

Devon's chest puffed out as he pulled himself more upright. "I did. I decided to go back to the bar and confront him, man to man. And do you know what happened next?"

Lana shook her head.

"When I opened the bathroom door, there he was, standing right in front of me. Someone had thrown a drink in his face—"

Jeanie raised her hand. "That was me."

"Well done," he said, nodding appreciatively. "And he wanted to clean it off. He recognized me and called me by name. His tone was so taunting, I could feel myself shutting down, and then I felt the ring on my finger, and I just let loose. I told him everything I had gone through since he wrote those lies about me. It was so cathartic."

"How did he react?" Lana asked.

"Smug at first, but the more I talked, the more he seemed to hear me. In the end, he finally admitted that he did not set out to destroy me—that it was only business. That article was reprinted so often, he made thousands off of it. Which is why he kept writing those horrid follow-up pieces."

"Good for you, Devon!" Jeanie exclaimed and raised her orange juice up in a toast.

"Somehow hearing Guy admit that he had lied in those articles was more satisfying than winning the libel lawsuit." Devon looked around the table, beaming. "Best of all, I don't feel any bitterness eating away at my soul anymore. As soon as I told him how I felt, it was as if all of the negativity had left my body. It's the first time since that article was published that I don't feel horrible every second of the day. I feel like a free man."

"It's a miracle," Evelyn whispered.

Devon took his wife's hand and kissed it tenderly. "All thanks to you and your eagle eye. I still can't believe you found our lucky rings again."

Evelyn laughed. "Well, this is the place to come for Celtic jewelry."

"I am so glad I got the chance to tell Guy how I feel before he was killed. Otherwise, I probably would have carried around that emotional baggage for the rest of my life."

Evelyn's eyes snapped shut, and she seemed to be quivering, Lana noted. *That was an odd reaction to her husband's comments*, she thought.

"Did you see their confrontation?" Lana asked, figuring it would have been difficult to witness.

"I wish I had," Evelyn said and looked up to her husband. "It would have been cathartic for both of us to see Devon stand up to that horrible man. But I am so glad he had the chance and courage to tell Guy how he felt." She smiled warmly at him, but when she looked away, Lana swore she saw sadness in Evelyn's eyes. It must have been terribly difficult to see her husband's reputation and business destroyed, especially by falsehoods.

Randy stood up and clapped his hands together. "Hey, gang, our taxi is here. It's time to start our day!"

"Could you stop with the clapping?" Patrick muttered, holding his head.

"Leave him be, Pops—he's young and enthusiastic. It's great to see," Nina replied. "You on the other hand, are old and crotchety," she teased, wagging a finger playfully in front of his face.

Patrick Senior's eyes narrowed. "Just you wait until you reach my age. I feel like the world is spinning along like it always has, but I can't keep up anymore. It wears a man down."

"I hear ya, Dad," Paddy said, throwing an arm over his father's shoulders. "If you want to skip today's tours, that's fine by us. But I think you'll regret it."

"Oh? What is on the agenda today—more churches and parks?"

"Today are most of the activities I requested—a tour of the Guinness Storehouse, a visit to their experimental brewery in Saint James's Gate, and lunch at the Jameson Whiskey Distillery, followed by a tour and tasting session, of course."

Patrick's hands fell from his forehead as he sat up straight. "Are you pulling my leg? That sounds like the perfect day in Dublin. Well done, my boy." He clapped his son on the back. "Did you say experimental Guinness?"

Paddy shone brightly. "Yes, I did. I hope you will be able to enjoy it, despite your hangover."

"Hair of the dog is my favorite way to recover from a night out. Works every time." Patrick stood up and glanced around at the group. "What are we waiting for?"

"Excellent," Randy enthused. "Our taxi is right outside."

18

Confidential Sources

After her group's taxi pulled away from the hotel, Lana set off by foot for the offices of the *Dublin Chronicle*. Even though it was a long shot that anyone would talk to her about their recently deceased colleague, she couldn't sit around and do nothing. Lana was certain Jeremy, despite having been caught red-handed, had not killed Guy. He was not a violent man and would never risk doing anything that would take him away from his wife and children.

It took her a few wrong turns before she found the small blue door marking the entrance to the *Dublin Chronicle*. It took even longer for someone to answer the bell and buzz her upstairs.

Lana climbed the three flights of stairs up to the newspaper's main office. The entire floor of the old storehouse was filled with a plethora of desks arranged in groups of two and three. Behind each sat reporters ticking away at their articles, designers laying out pages on the computer, or sales personnel chattering away with clients.

It felt so familiar and welcoming that Lana momentarily missed being a part of a newspaper's team. Working so closely together had created what Lana thought would be lasting bonds. Unfortunately, she had learned the hard way that the connections were anything but permanent. Hers had been severed as soon as she was wrongly accused of libel. What had hurt most had been how her co-workers quickly agreed with the accusations and publicly shunned her, instead of telling the truth—that she had been a damn good reporter who always did her best to be truthful and honest.

"Welcome to the *Dublin Chronicle*. Can I help you?"

A young woman with hair the color of gold stood before Lana. Her warm reception snapped Lana back to the present day.

"Yes, you can." Lana looked more closely at the employees spread across the vast space until a colorful bob caught Lana's eye. "I was hoping to talk to that reporter over there—the woman with pink hair."

"Ah, yes, Colleen. Give me a moment, will ya?"

Seconds later, the reporter in question turned towards Lana and squinted, as if she was trying to place her. She walked over and held out a hand. "Colleen Murphy. What can I do for you?"

"Do you have a moment to talk—preferably somewhere more private?" Lana asked, looking around at the buzzing space. She wasn't concerned that someone would overhear them, but did not want to have to yell to be heard over all the background noise. And as a reporter, Colleen would be used to potential sources wanting to talk in private.

A tiny smile seemed to be forming on the woman's face. "Please follow me."

She led Lana to a small conference room and closed the door and window shades so they had more privacy. She sat down on one side of the table and gestured for Lana to take a seat across from her. After she did, Colleen leaned forward. "What story do you have to share with me today?"

"I am a tour guide leading a group from Seattle, Washington, through Dublin. We met last night, or rather, I noticed you at the pub we were at." Lana nodded to Colleen's hair.

The reporter sat back in her chair and looked at Lana with a hint of suspicion. "I did go out last night, but I don't recall seeing you."

"I don't know the name of the pub, but you came in with a few people, including one of your colleagues, Guy Smith. He was killed in the alleyway, and one of my clients had been arrested in connection with his murder."

Colleen shot forward in her chair. "Jeremy Tartal is one of the tourists in your group? He was the person caught standing over Guy, with blood on his hands. Correct?"

"Yes, that is true."

"Interesting. Let me guess—you don't think he did it?"

Lana jutted out her chin. "No, I do not. He had no motive. I get why the police took him in for questioning, but I don't understand why they arrested him. His wife, who is also one of my clients, said the police decided to take him into custody after they talked to reporters from this newspaper. I was curious to know why."

Colleen locked eyes with Lana, obviously watching her reaction. "Why do you care?"

"They seem like incredibly nice people and are friends of the tour company's owner. She wants me to follow up because she doesn't trust the local police to search for another suspect, now that they have Jeremy in custody," Lana fibbed. She didn't want to admit that she and Jeremy were close, for fear that Colleen would dismiss her questions as nothing more than a desperate attempt to set her friend free. Which, in fact, they were.

"That's rather harsh! I can imagine it would be tempting for some police departments to let a tourist take the fall. However, here in Ireland we do try to figure out who really committed the crime, not just slap any sucker with a jail sentence," Colleen reasoned.

"Of course," Lana soothed, trying quickly to backtrack. "I am not trying to imply that the Irish police would intentionally allow Jeremy to pay for a crime he didn't commit. But if it meant sparing a local, they might consider the case closed, if they can prove Jeremy could have done it. Don't you think?"

Colleen was silent. Lana took it as a sign that she was considering her words, but apparently, the reporter just wanted to try a different tactic. "Jeremy's lawyers should be privy to the information we shared with the police. Why don't you ask them?"

"Trust me, I will, when I get the chance. Tell you what, if you don't want to share your findings with me, I accept that. But while I'm here, I was hoping you could tell me what happened that night, from your perspective."

Colleen eyed Lana warily.

"It was such a chaotic night that I lost sight of a few of my clients right before Guy's body was found." Lana bowed her head and lowered her voice, wanting to break eye contact for fear that Colleen would be able to tell that she was lying. "I have reason to believe another one of them had a motive for murdering Guy, but I don't know the exact chain of events. Did anyone else come up to you or your group that night?"

"Alright, I'll play along. We had all worked late and wanted to grab a pint before we pissed off for home. As soon as we entered the pub, Guy had a verbal squabble with Jeremy, and then a crazy woman splashed a drink across his face."

"Did Guy say how he knew Jeremy or the woman?"

"We had all heard about Jeremy before, and how his lies had made it impossible for Guy to find work stateside. But when we asked why that lady threw a drink on him, he said some women were impossible to please and refused to elaborate. I don't know what her name is, but based on his reaction, I would guess that they had once dated."

"The crazy woman is Jeanie Schwartz—she is also on my tour," Lana said as she cheered internally, glad to hear someone else confirm her own suspicions. She would definitely have to ask Jeanie about her relationship with Guy. "Did he say something about anyone else in the pub?"

Colleen paused and her eyes shot to the right. "Na. Guy tried wiping the drink off, but we didn't have enough napkins. Jeanie must have tossed a whole pint on him. He asked me to buy him a lager, then nipped off to the loo. We were still working on our first round when we heard the screams. Most of the patrons rushed out, but we stayed long enough to figure out that the murder victim was indeed our Guy. The police shooed us out when our paper's crime reporter showed up."

"And none of you went to the bathroom to check on him?"

"Na, he wasn't gone that long. Maybe five minutes—if that," Colleen replied.

Lana nodded, taking in Colleen's words while she thought of more questions to ask. "What kind of person was he?"

Colleen leaned back in her chair, considering her answer. "He antagonized everyone he worked with, but to potential sources he was a gentleman. It was all show, of course. I'm no psychologist, but he seemed to be a good manipulator who had a knack for getting people to trust him enough to let their guard down and reveal secrets that they wouldn't normally tell a stranger."

"Did he have other enemies—I mean, people that may have wanted to physically harm him? Was he the kind of guy people wanted to murder? Maybe someone who was not happy with what he had written about them?"

Colleen laughed. "I couldn't answer that. Guy was not the easiest person to work with, but he was never one of those lads who liked to pick fights with other patrons, despite his bluster at the bar last night."

When Lana paused to think of her next question, Colleen leaned forward. "Since you are here, what can you tell me about Jeremy Tartal?"

"He is an editor for the *Snoqualmie Gazette*; it's a regional newspaper in Washington state. Jeremy is the one who figured out that Guy had lied about his sources and exposed him as a fraud. News spread quickly, and Guy wasn't able to find work in the United States after that."

"Which is why he came to work for the *Dublin Chronicle*," Colleen finished.

Lana started at her answer. "Yes. Wait, you know about Guy's fake sources? How did he get a job here?"

"We are a sensationalist tabloid, and his cousin is the editor-in-chief. Besides, our style of reporting attracts a large circulation, which makes the team of lawyers we have on retainer cost effective."

"Aha," Lana whispered, finally understanding how Guy managed to find work as a reporter, despite his background. His boss was family.

"And Jeremy's wife, Kitty Tartal? What do you know about her? You said she is also a friend of the tour company's owner."

Lana's face scrunched up. "How do you know about Kitty?"

"Guy kept banging on about a story he was working on and mentioned a Kitty a few times. It took me a while to work out that he meant a person, not someone's pet."

Lana's ears perked up. If Guy had told Colleen about the article and why Kitty was a part of it, she would be several steps closer to finding out why the police had arrested Jeremy. It was her turn to lean forward and put on her biggest smile.

"I heard Guy tell Jeremy that the article would destroy his wife's career, but it wasn't clear why. She is a marketing assistant, not a top-level executive. How did Kitty fit into the story?"

Colleen's brow furrowed. "She is? Bugger, that is not good. Guy claimed otherwise in his article." She looked to the windows, as if she was worried one of her colleagues might be listening in.

"Since you have been so forthcoming, a few weeks ago Guy got all excited about a document he had received from a whistleblower. It was an organizational chart for a microbrewery based out of Seattle, Washington, called Firehouse Brewery. When we pressed him, he would only say that he knew Kitty Tartal's husband, but didn't mention how. According to his article, Kitty is a senior-level marketing manager at the brewery."

"No, that's not true. But why was Guy investigating Firehouse Brewery?"

"It's being acquired by EuroBeer, which is a new brewery based out of Ireland that is trying to establish itself as a major player in the European market. They have an investor with deep pockets and a mandate to expand rapidly. They have been buying up American microbreweries that win awards so they can produce their ales on a larger scale and distribute them here in Europe. Shortly after the microbreweries are acquired, they are closed and the staff fired. It's more profitable than a merger, at least, for EuroBeer. All they really want are the award-winning recipes."

"That is strange. Kitty is certain that her company is merging with EuroBeer, not being acquired by them. Her boss promised that everyone would keep their jobs."

Colleen sniggered. "A boss's promises don't mean much when there are millions on the line."

"Is that why the police arrested Jeremy? I still don't understand why this information would drive him to murder. If what you said about EuroBeer is true, then Kitty will lose her job as soon as the acquisition is approved, whether Guy published that article or not."

It was Colleen's turn to blush. "Jeremy was probably arrested on account of the role Guy attributed to Kitty in his article."

Lana sighed. "I don't understand."

"The focus of Guy's article was not the acquisition. According to his research notes and rough drafts, Firehouse Brewery had falsified their accounting records to make the company appear to be more profitable than it really is. That inflated their price, which, in fact, means they were committing corporate fraud."

"Wait a second. Kitty works for the marketing department, not in finance. Why would Guy have included her in his exposé?"

"According to the article he was writing, Kitty was responsible for crafting the company's deceptive marketing materials—things like newsletters, social media posts, and advertisements containing false claims that were designed to inflate the stock prices and mislead both stockholders and her fellow employees into believing the deal was a merger, not an acquisition."

"That's not true at all!" Lana roared, too late realizing that her reaction was extraordinary for someone who wasn't supposed to know Jeremy or Kitty well.

Colleen cocked her head. "So you are only their guide—not a friend?"

Lana blushed. "Well, maybe I didn't tell the entire truth about that…"

The reporter smiled as she rose and crossed to the conference room door. "Come on, I'll show you the files I found. Maybe you can help me separate the truth from the lies."

Lana skipped after her, thrilled the woman was being so generous. Colleen led them to her desk and opened up a folder on her computer marked "Guy."

"My editor asked me to take a look at Guy's files to see how far along he was with his article, as well as check to see if I could finish it, using the notes he had left behind. Our tech guy reset his password so I could access his files. Because we share desks, we all have our own password-protected space on the newspaper's server to add our stories and research files to, so we can access them from anywhere in the building. When I was reviewing his initial drafts, I noticed several strange footnotes that didn't seem to be related to the article. It took me a while to puzzle it out, but I'm fairly certain it is a code he was using to keep track of which sources he was citing in the article were real and which were fabricated."

"He did what?" Lana shrieked, then immediately ducked down when the newsroom turned to look. "That's what got him in so much trouble back in the States. Or does your boss not care about journalistic integrity?"

Colleen chuckled. "Even sensationalist newspapers have their limits. Our editor wouldn't appreciate getting pulled into court. And Guy's article would have been fact-checked before publication, so I don't know if this ever would have made it into the newspaper. However, the police were quite interested in reading Guy's rough drafts, even though they know that he was stretching the truth."

"If that's the case, why do you think he bothered fabricating all of these lies?"

"To save his job," Colleen said.

That stopped Lana short. "What do you mean?"

"His cousin convinced the newspaper's owner to pay Guy a royal salary. He liked to call Guy his golden boy, but so far as I can tell, he didn't write anything truly extraordinary during the four months that he worked here. Rumor had it, he was about to get sacked, at least until he came up with this big scoop about the microbrewery. Guy claimed a whistleblower sent him a stack of confidential documents and emails that proved Firehouse Brewery had been manipulating its worth so that EuroBeer would pay much more for it. Guy kept banging on about how it was going to be the scoop of the year, but he refused to share any specifics, even with our boss."

"That explains why he was writing an article about a Seattle-based company," Lana said.

"Indeed. It was a switch for us, but the tie-in to EuroBeer made it newsworthy for our audience."

Lana felt a sinking feeling in the pit of her stomach. "You aren't going to publish the article, are you?"

"Not as Guy wrote it. We are going to publish about Firehouse's attempts to inflate their price; Guy had secured enough emails and confidential documents to back up that claim. But we couldn't include his accusations about Kitty even if our editor-in-chief wanted to—I found no evidence that she was involved with the deal or fraud. It is clear to me now that Guy made up these lies because he blamed Jeremy for ruining his career—which is why he was going after Kitty."

Lana breathed a sigh of relief. "Thanks for being so honest with me."

"Before you go, you mentioned another guest of yours had a grudge against Guy. What is their name?"

Lana thought on Devon and how Guy's article had destroyed his businesses, as well as Mitch and the LowDown Records fiasco. She still didn't know enough to point the finger at anyone else, no matter how much she wanted to see Jeremy go free. "It's more a strong suspicion than that I've found definitive proof," Lana said. "Tell you what, if I learn more, you will be the first to know."

Colleen searched Lana's face, then nodded slowly. "Alright. I'll hold you to it."

"Would it be possible to get a copy of Guy's files about Firehouse Brewery?" Lana asked.

"I already gave them to the police so I don't mind sending you a copy via email," Colleen said.

"Great." Lana wrote down her email address, then moved aside, making room for Colleen to reach the keyboard. A few moments later, her phone pinged as it announced the receipt of Guy's notes and rough drafts.

Lana held out her hand. "I cannot thank you enough for your help today."

"It's my pleasure. I hope our conversation helps your friend." Colleen glanced at her wristwatch, then sprung out of her chair. "Bugger! I didn't realize it was so late. I have an interview to conduct in a few minutes. If I have any questions about Jeremy or Kitty, can I call you?"

Lana pursed her lips, hating the fact that her friend's arrest was a newsworthy item. "Of course. You've been so generous with your time and information. I'm happy to help, if you need it."

"Excellent. Ta for that," Colleen said and shot her a smile before speeding off to her next appointment.

19

Late for Lunch

"Holy cow," Lana mumbled as she sank back into her hotel room's comfortable armchair. After an enlightening conversation with Colleen, she had rushed back to the hotel to read through Guy's notes about the Firehouse Brewery article, before she had to rejoin her tour group.

The more she read, the madder she grew. The corporate fraud would have been sensational enough; there was no need to include Kitty. Yet after she finished reading all of the notes and Guy's rough drafts, she still was not convinced this article would have damaged her career. Guy's lies were fairly easy to disprove, meaning it would have made him look bad, not Kitty. Wouldn't it have?

Lana's stomach began to rumble at the same moment her phone rang.

"How are you doing?" Randy asked.

"Great. I found a reporter at the *Dublin Chronicle* willing to talk, and I was just reading through some of the information she gave me," Lana responded then looked at the time, grimacing when she realized it was already twelve o'clock. She had promised to meet the group in time for lunch. "It looks like I am running a bit late. How are things going with you?"

"Things are well. Everyone is enjoying themselves thoroughly—especially the O'Tooles," Randy said with a laugh. "I just wanted to let you know that we are running a little late, as well, but are still heading over to Teeling Distillery's café for lunch before the whiskey tour. Not that this bunch needs any more to drink."

"Thanks for holding down the fort, Randy. I'm walking out of the hotel now and should be at the restaurant before you are."

"Great. We will see you soon!"

20

Whiskey and Bacon

Could Devon be the killer? Lana wondered as she watched him strolling hand in hand with his wife. He was a different man since his confrontation with Guy, that was for certain—far more confident and self-assured. When he leaned over to whisper into his wife's ear, whatever he said brought a grin to her face that radiated love and happiness.

After a rushed, yet delicious, lunch, they entered the Teeling Distillery for a tour and whiskey tasting. Lana had missed this morning's excursions, but based on their frivolity, she figured that everyone had already had plenty to drink.

The distillery was a sensory overload of sweet scents and loud machinery. As soon as their Irish host began explaining the whiskey-making process, it was clear to Lana that neither Devon nor Evelyn was interested. Her mind couldn't let Guy's article about the art dealers go. When the couple lagged at the back, Lana saw her chance to hear Devon's side of the story.

"Hi, how are you two doing?" Lana asked.

Evelyn chuckled. "Oops, is it that obvious that we aren't really interested in this tour?"

Lana blushed. "It's okay—this week is quite a mishmash of excursions. But it's been fun so far, right?"

"Heck, yes! Though I have to say, neither one of us want to take part in the whiskey tasting after this tour. We would rather see Francis Bacon's art studio. It's been rebuilt in the Hugh Lane Art Gallery."

"That sounds fascinating! I read about how art conservators meticulously documented his entire studio after his death, then moved it from London to Dublin—"

"Even the dust!" Devon broke in.

"What an incredible monument to such an important artist," Lana agreed.

"Bacon always said he would come back to Dublin when he was dead. I guess they made his wish come true," Devon laughed.

"Friends of mine were here last year and said it's quite chaotic, but is a captivating insight into Bacon's mind," Evelyn added.

"Can I arrange a taxi or entrance tickets for you?"

"Evelyn has already bought the tickets, but a ride would be wonderful, thank you," Devon said.

"It's my pleasure," Lana said. "Before I do, could we talk privately for a moment?"

They gave her a puzzled look, but did follow Lana as she walked a few steps farther away from their group.

"Is something wrong?" Evelyn asked.

"Not at all. I am not trying to put you on the spot, but I did meet with a local reporter this morning, in order to find out more about Guy and his beef with Jeremy."

Evelyn's brow furrowed, and Devon looked to the ground. "We are sorry to hear about your friend," she said. "But what does Jeremy have to do with us?"

"She showed me the rough draft of the story he was writing about Kitty, and it was full of lies," Lana said as she looked to Devon. "Guy has done that before, hadn't he?"

Evelyn paled considerably, and Devon seemed to be shaking. When they remained silent, Lana pushed, "I read all the articles Guy wrote about your business and the other art dealers, as well as those documenting how your legal team disproved them as lies. Is Guy's article why you went bankrupt?"

"Yes," Devon hissed. "He destroyed my business and reputation. Within days of the initial article's publication, all of my regular clients canceled their viewing appointments, and several buyers returned their recent acquisitions and demanded their money back. I simply did not have enough cash to deal with it all at the same time. It broke me—literally."

He paused to wipe a tear from his eye. "As soon as the criminal investigation was dropped, the other art experts mentioned in the article and I immediately sued the newspaper for defamation, but the damage had already done. Too many people had read and believed Guy's original article. Even if our lawyers finally win our case against him, I don't think I will ever be able to own a gallery again. My reputation has been obliterated, and there is nothing I can do to change that."

"That article crushed him, yet nothing in it was true!" Evelyn roared. "Devon did everything he could to guarantee the authenticity of those paintings. That's why he had them examined by two experts, instead of one. It's been a year now, and the falsehoods in that article still haunt Devon. Not only did it destroy his gallery and restoration business, but bookstores also refuse to stock any of his nonfiction works on art, which were a sizable portion of his income."

"Devon, did you come here to get your revenge on Guy?"

"No!" Evelyn answered for him. "We needed to get away, and when Dotty called and asked if we were interested, I figured this was as good a place as any. We had talked a lot about coming here one day, because of our ancestral ties and our interest in Celtic art. But it was simply coincidence that we came on this tour instead of another. If Dotty had asked if we wanted to take a tour of Timbuktu at a discount, we probably would have said yes."

Lana shook her head, trying to wrap her mind around the horrible coincidence of their choice of location. "And you didn't know Guy was living in Ireland?"

Devon snorted. "Trust me, if we had known that Guy was in Dublin, we never would have come. He is the reason why we wanted to get away!"

Lana nodded in sympathy, wondering whether what they said was indeed true. Didn't Devon say that as long as Guy lived, he would not feel free? If he wanted to take his revenge on the reporter, then coming here on an organized tour would be a great cover.

Devon claimed his verbal confrontation with Guy at the pub was enough to free him from the negativity eating at his soul. But it didn't bring his businesses back, nor did it restore his reputation. She could imagine it took a lot of courage to stand up to the man who destroyed your life. If he had gotten up the gumption to do it, would he have also been capable of taking it a step further and killing the object of his rage? It wouldn't give him his career back, but it may have provided the closure he needed to move on with his life. Since Guy's death, Devon had been a man reborn. And it was clear from Evelyn's reaction that this new and improved Devon was the man she had once fallen in love with.

Yet Lana knew firsthand how devastating it was to be falsely accused of a crime and what that could do to you. A swell of sympathy overwhelmed her when she looked again to her guests. Having the chance to tell Guy how he felt could certainly explain the positive changes in his attitude towards life. *Devon isn't the killer*, she thought.

Still, he did have the strongest motive, so far as Lana knew. She owed it to Jeremy to push him a little further and see whether he snapped. "Devon, you told the police that you and Evelyn were on your way to the bathroom when Guy was killed. But the next day, you told us all that you had confronted him after you left the toilet. And that Evelyn was not there to hear it."

Devon closed his eyes as he realized his mistake.

"Where were you two really when Guy died? Did either of you harm him? Or see who did?"

Both suspects began violently shaking their heads. "After Guy and I ran into each other, I pulled him out into the alleyway so I could let loose without the pub's staff stepping in. After we finished talking, or rather, after I finished dumping on Guy, I walked off into the night to clear my head. It felt great to finally tell him how I felt, but it was confusing, too. I needed a chance to process my emotions before I rejoined Evelyn. When I came back around to the front of the pub, police cars were pulling up to the curb. I swear Guy was alive when I left him in the alleyway. Why would I return to the bar, otherwise? I could have called Evelyn and told her to get out of there, or waited for her back at the hotel."

"Then why didn't you just tell the police the truth?"

"Because I didn't want to place myself at the scene of the crime. I was afraid they would take me in for questioning, too, and I do have a strong motive for wanting to harm him. Even though I did not," Devon said quite emphatically.

"Did Guy go back inside the pub when you walked off?"

"He did open the door, but closed it and lit up a cigarette, instead. Since you can't smoke inside, I assume he stayed outside to finish it."

Lana thought back to the crime scene. The alleyway was filthy and the garbage cans overflowing. She didn't recall seeing a cigarette smoldering next to his body, but there could have easily been one.

"Look, I understand your friend has been taken into custody, but I did not harm Guy," Devon said, his tone testy. "My art restoration business and gallery are bankrupt, my publisher won't return my calls, and no one wants to book me in for a lecture. It's a good thing we paid off our mortgage and cars years ago, otherwise we probably would have lost those, as well. I don't see how anyone could hurt me any further. And killing Guy would not have restored my reputation or businesses."

"Do you have any more questions, or should we catch up to the others?" Evelyn asked.

Lana startled when she checked her watch. "Uh-oh. I bet the tour is about to end and we missed all of it."

Evelyn waved it off. "That's alright. We aren't big whiskey drinkers, but we are art lovers. Could you call that taxi for us now? We will be waiting out front." She took her husband's hand and the two of them walked away without looking back.

"Will do," Lana said and dialed the cab company her boss recommended. After she'd arranged their transportation, Lana scurried to catch up with the rest of her group.

Who else could it be? she wondered as she considered her other guests' motives. The truth was, she didn't know enough about them to know whether they had a great reason to want to harm Guy. *Time to rectify that situation,* Lana thought, vowing to do just that during their next break.

21

Cooking the Books

After a day of too much alcohol and hearty food, Lana cajoled her giddy guests back to the hotel for a two-hour break before dinner. As much as she wanted to jump back online and find out more about Guy and her other guests straightaway, she needed to first have a long talk with Kitty. Lana was fairly certain Guy's article was going to upset her, and she preferred to have this conversation in person.

Lana knocked on Kitty's door soon after they returned. An hour earlier, Kitty had messaged her to say that she was leaving the police station to return to the hotel. Lana didn't know whether that was a good or bad sign.

When Kitty finally opened the door, her face was puffy and red. Tears still stained both cheeks, despite her attempts to dry her eyes. "Come in, Lana," she mumbled as she stepped back to let her inside.

Lana wrapped her friend up in a hug and pulled her down onto the edge of the king-sized bed. "Sweetie, I'm so sorry about all of this. We both know Jeremy didn't do this. What did the lawyer say?"

"It's going to be tough to prove his innocence. He was caught standing over the body with Guy's blood on his hands. The pub has video surveillance, but they don't have a camera hanging in the back alley. The lawyer is talking about hiring a private investigator to look for another potential motive or suspect, which makes me nervous, frankly. The police should be doing that, but apparently they aren't too motivated to look for another."

Kitty began to sob again. "I don't know what I'm going to do! I already called his parents and brought them up to speed."

"Oh, no—your daughters! What are you going to tell them?"

"We agreed to keep it from the girls for now, at least until the official trip is over. I don't want to have to tell them that their dad has been arrested, especially for something he didn't do!"

Lana's heart went out to Kitty. "I promise to do all I can to help you. I did already visit the newspaper Guy worked for and found out some interesting information."

"Good, I could use some positive news right about now."

Lana winced. "I don't know how positive it is. What exactly has your boss told you about the merger?"

Kitty rolled her eyes. "What does this have to do with Jeremy?"

Lana drew in her breath, knowing it was important to be honest with her friend, yet dreading being the bearer of bad news. Kitty was already dealing with enough as it was, without having to add her employer's deception to the list. "It appears Firehouse Brewery's accounting department cooked the books to make it appear as if it was worth more than it really is."

When Kitty started to protest, Lana talked over her. "The reporter at the *Dublin Chronicle* sent me a copy of all of Guy's research notes. He had a plethora of confidential documents in his possession that confirm Firehouse was committing fraud. Guy also had proof that the marketing department had been sending out misleading information to stockholders, which also helped to increase the value of the stock and company. Guy's article implies this was all done to increase the company's worth so they could demand more from EuroBeer during the acquisition negotiations."

Kitty shook her head. "I can't believe it. They were already one of the most profitable microbreweries on the West Coast. But, as disappointing as it is to hear that my employer is a crook, none of this has anything to do with me."

Lana cringed, almost sorry that she had to tell her the truth. "At a certain point in Guy's article, fact and fiction part ways. You are specifically mentioned as having been the mastermind behind the company's deceptive marketing practices. Guy claimed that, as a senior marketing manager, you crafted the intentionally misleading materials sent to your shareholders, which helped to inflated the stock price."

"That doesn't make any sense! I am a marketing assistant, not a mastermind of anything!" Kitty yelled, then froze.

"Oh, no." She sank back down on the bed and buried her head in her hands. "They set me up."

Lana stiffened. "What are you not telling me?"

"After the board of directors returned from Ireland, my boss called me into her office and told me they had decided to promote me to a senior marketing manager. I am going to begin a six-month training program in a few weeks, but they gave me the title and raise immediately. My boss claimed it was easier for human resources to have the promotion take effect at the end of February, instead of waiting until I had actually begun the training."

"That is a big step up from assistant marketer," Lana murmured.

"It was quite a shock, certainly. But my manager made me feel like they had chosen to promote me because they believed in me. They said that after the merger, they would need a larger marketing staff and wanted to prepare some of their better candidates for the role. I was flattered they thought so highly of me, especially since I only started working there a few months ago."

"True, though your promotion could be misinterpreted as a reward for your role in the corporate fraud. That is what Guy seems to be implying in his article."

"I swear I didn't know about any deceptive marketing materials or fraud the company may be perpetrating! If Firehouse Brewery did cook their books in order to deceive their investors, I had nothing to do with it," Kitty wailed.

"The police might think that Jeremy killed Guy to save your career. No reporter, no article. And his colleague did say that Guy refused to share any information about his exposé with anyone," Lana said quietly.

"This is a nightmare. How could Firehouse do this to me?" Kitty's shoulders heaved back and forth as sobs racked her body.

"When did they promote you exactly?" Lana asked gently.

"The day after they returned from Dublin, so that would have been the first week in February. If they had promoted me before the trip, then I would have gone with them," Kitty said, then slapped her palm to her forehead. "Of course—they must have realized during the trip that they needed a scapegoat, and I was the newest hire."

Her head bent over, and Kitty released a cry that tore at Lana's soul.

"I couldn't believe it when they hired me. I had been searching for a job for months, and everyone turned me down as soon as they saw I had spent the last eight years raising the girls. I was so shocked and happy when Firehouse called me in for a second interview and then offered me a job on the spot! The human resources manager made it sound like they truly believed in me and my abilities. Or so I thought."

"Why would they have hired you to be their scapegoat on a deal that had not even happened yet?" Lana reasoned.

"They were already working with EuroBeer on the merger when I joined the company. They must have hired me because they figured I wasn't smart enough to discover their deceit. And they were right—I didn't; that's what hurts the most. Maybe I should just stay at home and focus on the kids."

"What? Are you kidding me? It's not your fault that they were committing fraud! How damaging would the article have been to your career, do you think?" Lana asked.

"Honestly, I don't know. But it doesn't matter now. If Guy's allegations are true, then no one will have a job after this is over. Darn it!"

"You can always find another job," Lana reasoned.

"This hasn't helped to strengthen my resume, that's for sure."

"You are resourceful and smart; I know you will find something else," Lana said, knowing her words would not lessen Kitty's pain right now.

When her friend began to tear up again, Lana pulled her in for a hug. "Try not to think about it too much, right now. We need to focus our attention on Jeremy. He did not do this—we both know that. Now all we have to do is prove it."

22

Pinstripe Mafia

Maybe I'm going about this the wrong way, Lana thought, as she returned to her hotel room after comforting Kitty as best as she could. Other than Devon, she hadn't found any articles written by Guy in which one of her guests or their companies were explicitly mentioned. But she hadn't investigated her guests' backgrounds to see whether they knew Guy another way.

If it was not Jeremy or Devon, who else had reason to kill Guy Smith? Lana wondered, tapping her open notebook with her pen. She wrote all of her guests' names down, determined to find out more about each of them.

At the top of her list was Jeanie the genealogist. Based on her client's word choices and reaction to Guy's presence, not to mention what Colleen had said, Lana would not be surprised if he was the former lover Jeanie had hoped to rekindle a romance with. Yet Guy was clearly not interested in her. If Jeanie had flown over here to be with him, only to be rejected, would she have been mad enough to have bashed him on the head with a leprechaun statue?

Lana powered up her laptop and typed in Jeanie's name into Facebook. Sure enough, one look at Jeanie's social media confirmed her suspicions. Based on the many photos of them kissing and cuddling, it appeared that her genealogist client and Guy had dated for almost a year. Yet four months ago, Guy disappeared from Jeanie's social media timeline, and there was no more mention of him, until a week before this trip commenced. Jeanie had posted a photo of a wedding dress in a suitcase, with two gold rings resting on the veil. The caption read: "It still fits! Expect to hear wedding bells ringing later this month."

Lana's mouth dropped open. No wonder Jeanie threw a drink in Guy's face. Here she thought they were going to get married, and he rejected her outright the moment he set eyes on her. *That had to hurt,* she thought, wondering how far Jeanie would have gone to get her revenge on Guy. She might be pushy and dramatic, but she didn't seem to be the murdering type. And she had openly flirted with Mitch, their young guides, and even Patrick Senior, despite claiming to be here to rekindle an old romance.

Yet she had flown over here to see Guy, despite her terrible motion sickness, and she was close to the alleyway door when he was killed. She and Guy did have a brief conversation moments before he was killed, and whatever he had said caused Jeanie to throw a drink in his face, so it must have been bad. If he had rejected her again, would she have killed him, given the chance? Bludgeoning someone to death seemed more like something a man would do, but if the crime was indeed committed in the heat of the moment, perhaps the killer simply used the first heavy object they came across?

How Lana wished she had paid more attention to her guests' comings and goings in the moments before Guy was murdered, as well as their table and the souvenirs underneath it.

When her timer went off, reminding Lana it was time to meet her guests in the lobby, she was still flipping through Jeanie's social media. What troubled her most was how happy both she and Guy seemed so be. What had happened to them?

Lana knew quite well that no relationship was perfect—her own failed marriage attested to that. But there was usually a reason for a couple to part. And Lana couldn't wait to get Jeanie alone and find out why she and Guy had broken up.

She shut down her computer and skipped down to the lobby, wondering what state of being her guests were going to be in. They were spread around the lobby and most seemed to be suffering from a hangover.

Only Evelyn and Devon were chipper and bright. He had an arm thrown over his wife's shoulders and was whispering in her ear. Whatever he was saying, Evelyn was reveling in the attention. Lana was truly shocked to see how different his attitude and posture were now, in comparison to the first day of the tour. It was as if he had come alive again.

Unsurprisingly, Paddy and Patrick were in pretty bad shape, both holding their heads in their hands while Nina looked on in disgust. Lana wanted to dart over to Jeanie and ask about the photos she had found, but Nina caught her eye instead.

"Can I dump these two somewhere? Neither one of them can hold their liquor anymore."

"Not all of us had years of practice while traveling around with their band, Nina," Patrick growled, then moaned, "I think I better skip the dinner. Could I order room service, instead?"

"Oh, Pops. What are we going to do with you?" Nina looked to her husband, who was in as sad a shape as his father. "I don't care how you're feeling, Paddy, but you are going with me to The Hairy Lemon Pub. It was my suggestion, after all. And from what Mitch tells me, we are guaranteed to see a great band or two."

"I promised you I would. You know I'm good for my word."

Nina nodded. "Why don't I take your dad back upstairs and order him some food?"

"I think that's a good idea," Paddy said and squeezed his eyes shut. "Could you get me an aspirin while you're up there?"

"Anything for you, love." Nina kissed her husband gently on the head before holding out an arm to her father-in-law. "Shall we?"

"I don't care what Paddy says about you, Nina. You are good people," Patrick said and winked at his son.

"Trust me—you don't want to know what we say about you in the still of the night," Nina cackled as she propelled her father-in-law towards the elevators.

Paddy leaned back into his chair and closed his eyes. As much as she wanted to talk to Jeanie, she was also quite curious to learn more about the article Guy had been writing about Firestone Brewery. Lana knew so little about finances and mergers that she could not gauge what its true effect on Kitty's career would have been.

Lana debated letting her client be, but her desire to move forward with her investigation weighed heavily on her mind. They wouldn't be able to have a normal conversation at the pub, and the O'Tooles were spending most of tomorrow visiting their ancestral home. It was now or never.

She sat down in the chair Nina had just vacated. "Hi, Paddy. Are you enjoying yourself so far?"

"Heck, yes!" he exclaimed then groaned. "This hangover is not pleasant, but it's not my fault. The Irish are more charming and welcoming than I ever could have imagined. From all of Dad's stories, I half-expected them all to be evil leprechauns focused on tricking me out of my money." Paddy blushed. "Sorry about the leprechaun remark. Dad never did have anything good to say about Ireland. How is it going with your friend Jeremy?"

"Not so good, to be honest. From what the lawyer told his wife, the police haven't found any other suspects. You are an accountant, correct?"

Paddy straightened at the mention of his occupation. "Yes, for thirty-one years and counting."

"I have a strange financial question for you, but I assure you it relates to Jeremy's case."

Paddy folded his hands over his belly. "Shoot."

"Is it possible for a marketing department to manipulate stock prices by sending out false information to their shareholders? And could such deceptive communications be intentionally used to raise the value of a company's worth—for example, if they are negotiating a merger?" Lana asked.

"You better believe it," Paddy bellowed. "The media always blames the pinstripe mafia when stock prices or companies' net worths are manipulated, but marketing strategies are far more often to blame these days."

Lana's eyebrows knitted together. "Let's back up a minute. What is the pinstripe mafia?"

"It's a derogatory name the media gave to bankers, lawyers, and accountants. I'm not saying that there are no bad eggs in my profession; financial statement manipulation remains an ongoing problem in corporate America. But most of us do our utmost to remain above board and explicitly follow the letter of the law."

"Oh, okay." Lana realized how sensitive a subject this must be for him. "But I still don't understand how marketers could influence stock prices or inflate a company's net worth."

Paddy blew out his cheeks. "People believe whatever a corporation tells them and rarely stop to question the accuracy or authenticity of their claims. Social media and the rise of alternative facts have made it even easier for companies to widely circulate falsified reports online. Just look at what happens when a company posts about amazing financial results on its social media or announces it is about to launch an incredible new product. The posts go viral, and the share prices skyrocket. But what if there is no new product or the financial results were far less sunny than presented?"

Paddy leaned back and crossed one leg over the other as he waited for Lana to answer.

"The stock prices plummet?" she ventured.

"Precisely. No one takes the time to do their research anymore. As soon as the reports are proved to be fake news, the stock prices crash, and everyone who invested too late loses a bunch of money."

Paddy suddenly leaned forward, his eyes sparkling. "But you better believe that whoever leaked that false information made a fortune before the truth came out. It's all manipulated, but do the marketing departments get investigated? Almost never. Everyone blames the financial department. Even in films about Wall Street, we are always portrayed as the evildoers."

Lana's eyes grew increasingly wide as his tirade continued. She had obviously hit a nerve. "I had no idea. You are absolutely correct—it's not something you see in films or hear about much in the media. But let's say a reporter was about to publish an article about the use of deceptive marketing practices to manipulate the company's value. If the marketing manager was named in the article, would their career suffer for it, do you think? Or is it something that that person could sweep under the rug?"

"I recently read in the *Harvard Business Review* that misleading marketing strategies have destroyed more shareholder value—and probably more careers—than shoddy accounting or fiscal practices ever have. If a marketing executive intentionally manipulated their shareholders, then yes, I think it would be incredibly difficult for that person to ever find work again."

Lana responded with as much respect as she could muster, "You have opened my eyes to a whole new world of deceit. Thanks for sharing your insights with me."

Internally, however, she was groaning. According to what Paddy had just told her, the accusations Guy was going to publish about Kitty would have destroyed her budding career. Even if she could later prove that she was not involved with the merger or the writing of the marketing materials, it wouldn't matter. The damage would have been done, just as it was in Devon's case. Once something is published, it is incredibly difficult to expunge it from the hearts and minds of millions of readers.

But did Jeremy know that Guy's article would destroy his wife's chance at success? He was not an accountant. But he was Kitty's husband, and having Guy threaten her in any way would have made him blind with rage. Lana supposed it didn't really matter whether Jeremy knew what damage the article would have done. The police would assume he did. The false accusations Guy included in it were probably enough to convince them that Jeremy had murdered the reporter to prevent its publication.

Lana rose just as Nina returned to the lobby and brought her husband two aspirin. "Here you go, babe. I hope these help."

23

Breaking Up Is Hard To Do

After Nina returned to the lobby, their group headed out to the awaiting taxi and sped off towards The Hairy Lemon Pub for a traditional meal and music.

"Is that the bar?" Paddy asked as their cab stopped close to the front entrance.

The green and yellow nineteenth-century house standing before them had been converted into a pub that was renowned for its Irish foods and as hosting the best *trad*, or open mic, sessions in Dublin. Mitch had already told them about the excellent bands he had heard a few nights earlier, so they were all prepped to hear the best of what the city had to offer. Given their love of live music, Lana was not surprised that both Nina and Mitch wanted to come here. She was, however, a bit shocked that Mitch did not have his guitar with him.

Yet, once they stepped inside, she understood Mitch's reluctance to bring his instrument. The vibe in the crowded pub was already a bit rowdy when they stepped inside, and it only increased in intensity as the night wore on. The Guinness flowed heavily, and most patrons were kicking up their heels and tapping their way across the tabletops before her group had finished their meal.

Their dinner—a traditional Irish stew—was to die for. Lana had always been a fan of stews, but this was next level. A platter, upon which two large bowls and a thick slab of bread rested, was set before her. In one bowl, peeled potatoes, thick slices of carrots, onion, and celery, and chunks of beef floated in a pool of bouillon. Its richness was the perfect antidote for this chilly weather. Bowl two contained another potato, this one baked and topped with a mountain of butter, sour cream, and chives.

After their waitresses cleared their tables, a new group of musicians took to the small podium in the back of the room. It seemed as if every pub, restaurant, and café in Dublin had a raised platform somewhere on the premises. Lana loved how integrated live music was into the social scene.

"It's incredible that we don't have to pay every time a band plays," Mitch shouted to Nina.

"Good thing for me that free music isn't normal in Seattle," she laughed. "But playing so often is a great way for a band to advertise and gain name recognition. We have to go back to Grafton Street again and listen to more of the buskers."

"That is an excellent idea. Too bad that you have to have a permit to play on the street, otherwise I would have been right there along with them," Mitch laughed, then closed his eyes and listened for a moment, before singing along. His rough voice was perfectly suited for the melody and its lilting qualities made Lana's heart sing.

"You have a beautiful voice," she said, hoping he wouldn't stop singing. Luckily, he continued. After the song ended and the crowd broke out into applause, she asked, "How do you know that song?"

"I'm a big fan of Irish folk music. My neighbor grew up in Ireland and played the fiddle. He taught me many of the classics he grew up with, and those melodies and lyrics help to inspire my own work."

"I'm glad to hear you are still recording. Say, I hope this doesn't seem too intrusive, but I read about LowDown Records recently and how the owner embezzled funds from their musicians. I heard you mention that you were also on that label. Did you know that Guy wrote the original article that exposed their illegal practices?"

Mitch's eyes widened to saucers, and he fell back into his chair. "You are joking. No, I had no idea he was the one. The accounting department kept making up excuses as to why our royalty checks were several months late, but we had no idea that management was stealing from us. It's through the newspapers that I found out about LowDown's illegal activities, but I didn't pay attention to who wrote the initial investigative piece. The story was covered in every paper and television news program the next day. If I had known that Guy had broken the story, I would have bought him a pint."

Mitch's reaction made Lana's head spin. Here she thought Mitch might have killed Guy out of revenge for destroying his livelihood, but it appeared that nothing could be further from the truth. "Excuse me? I thought you would have been upset, not happy to shake his hand."

"Why would I be upset with Guy? He did all of the musicians who worked for them a favor. They were stealing from us—I am glad they went under. Though it is frustrating that the owner skipped the country before he could be arrested"

Lana cocked her head at Mitch. "Still, it must have been really difficult starting over again. Especially with no royalty checks."

"Sure, I was mad about losing my label at first, but I'm earning more per sale now than I ever did with LowDown. Starting my own label was something I had been pondering for years but didn't have the guts to do. Looking back, I am truly grateful things happened this way. I thought I was getting a raw deal, but in fact it was the universe's way of forcing me to try a different path."

Mitch smiled, then turned his attention back to the musicians onstage as they started playing again. Instead of a ballad, their second and third songs were upbeat numbers that energized the crowd. When several patrons sprung back onto the bar and tables, Jeanie walked over to Lana. She almost seemed sad, which was a drastic change from her normal state of self-assuredness.

"I need some fresh air. I'm going to step outside for a minute. Is that alright?"

"Sure, Jeanie. Why don't I go with you?" Lana sprung up before her guest could say no.

She held open the door for her client, then stepped out onto the cobblestone streets. Lana took a deep breath of air and stared up at the plethora of stars. "What a beautiful night."

Jeanie murmured in agreement as she tilted her head up towards the heavens.

"How long did you and Guy date?"

Jeanie's head snapped down so quickly Lana was worried she might have whiplash.

"What? I never dated that hideous man!"

Lana pursed her lips at her client, wondering why the older woman continued to lie about her relationship with Guy. Was she ashamed to admit the truth? Or was she worried that Lana might think she had killed her former lover and would tell the police? It was time to find out. She turned her phone to Jeanie and showed her the photos she had found online. "Really? It sure looks like you two were pretty close."

Jeanie's eyes narrowed before she blew a lungful of air out through her nose. "We dated for a while. So what?"

"According to your social media, you dated for almost a year. And it looks like you were expecting him to propose. Why did you two break up?"

"Why were you checking out my social media?" she huffed. "The police already arrested your friend Jeremy. I'm not under investigation."

When Lana remained silent, the genealogist bit her lip and looked away. "The thing is, we didn't really break up. At least, I was not aware that we had. I thought we had a loving relationship and truly thought he was going to propose to me. We didn't share a home, but did spend most of the week together. Then one day he didn't show up when I expected him and didn't answer his phone. I thought maybe something horrible had happened to him, so I went to his apartment to check on him. When I got there, it was empty, and his landlord told me that he had moved to Dublin! He had even given his landlord thirty days' notice, which is more than I got. We had been dating for almost a year—can you believe the nerve?"

"That's horrible! And you haven't talked to him since then?"

"No," Jeanie moaned and turned her head upwards again. "He didn't answer a single email, telephone call, or text message. How could you up and leave someone you loved? We hadn't had a single argument or nasty disagreement; I truly thought he was the man I was going to spend the rest of my life with."

Lana thought back on the pudgy, balding man she had briefly met twice. Maybe he could be charming, but her encounters with him had been anything but pleasant. "Did he know you were coming to Dublin?"

Jeanie shook her head.

"So did you come over here expecting to get married? Or were you simply hoping for clarity and closure?"

Jeanie's shoulders slumped. "I don't know what I was thinking. Back home, I was so certain we were destined to be together. I thought if I could talk to him, we might have a chance at being a couple again. I knew he had been having trouble finding work and that whole thing with the newspaper editors severely injured his self-esteem. But I never would have guessed that he would leave without saying goodbye."

"I saw you throw a drink in his face, but did you get a chance to talk to him first?"

Jeanie sniffed. "Unfortunately, I did. He made clear that he didn't want to have anything more to do with me. He said it had been fun for a while, but he had grabbed this chance at a new career and wanted to start the rest of his life over, as well. It's as if I meant nothing to him! That's what hurt the most. I was so angry, I wanted to lash out at him, so I threw my drink in his face. That was a stupid move—alcohol here is a lot more expensive than back home."

Lana laid an arm over her shoulders, and Jeanie fell into her arms, sobbing inconsolably.

When she reined in her emotions, Lana tentatively asked. "So that flirting with Mitch and Patrick was…"

"Something to keep my mind off Guy, obviously." Jeanie straightened up and wiped the tears off her face. "You cannot seriously think I would be interested in either one of them. Mitch is a hippie, and Patrick is old enough to be my dad."

Though Jeanie vehemently denied it, it sure seemed like the genealogist was smitten with the folk singer and crotchety older man, as well as every local tour guide or bartender who looked her way.

Lana chose to not put her client further on the spot, instead focusing on her current state of being. "Are you going to be okay? Even though you and Guy were no longer a couple, I can imagine it hurts to know that he's gone."

Jeanie teared up again, though Lana suspected that these were fakes. "I'll find a way to go on."

"Great to know," Lana said as she pulled her jacket closer. "Say, it's pretty cold out here. I'm going to head back inside. Do you want to join me or stay outside a while longer?"

"I could use a drink. Shall we?" This time Jeanie held the door open for Lana.

The bar seemed even warmer and cozier after their chilly chat outside. Mitch was now onstage, playing a fast tune on a borrowed fiddle. Nina stood on a table, copying a local patron's stepdance moves, while Paddy and Patrick cheered the women on. Evelyn and Devon sat back watching the group with a smile on their faces.

"Is there room for one more?" Jeanie crooned as she climbed up onto an empty chair next to Nina's table.

"They aren't as stable as they look," Nina yelled down as Jeanie put one foot onto the table. Jeanie launched herself upwards, but before she made it, the table's top came loose from its base and tipped to one side, spilling her onto the floor and dumping Nina on top of her.

"Ow!" Jeanie yelped as Nina scrambled to get off of her. Unfortunately for the genealogist, her head glanced off another table when they fell, leaving her with a nasty cut on the left side of her scalp. Blood poured from the wound, quickly soaking her blouse.

"I'm going to be sick," Jeanie moaned and threw a hand to her forehead as she fell backwards. Paddy grabbed her as a bartender rushed over with a medical kit.

"You seem prepared," Nina exclaimed as the middle-aged Irishman expertly cleaned, then wrapped Jeanie's head wound.

"It's Ireland—she's not the first to fall off a table," he said, then addressed Jeanie. "Lucky for you, it's not that deep. Cuts to your head do tend to bleed a lot, but you shouldn't need stitches."

When Jeanie looked up at her savior, the pathetic grimace on her face turned into a coy smile. "I'm glad to have a man like you to take care of me." She squeezed his biceps, her grin intensifying when he blushed at her remark.

"Could I buy you a pint, as thanks?" she asked, fluttering her eyelashes furiously.

The man held out a hand and helped Jeanie up, kissing her hand before escorting her to the bar.

Lana chuckled to herself, glad to see that Jeanie had so quickly recovered from her injury and Guy's rejection. *She flew over to Dublin for love and she just might find it before the end of the week*, Lana thought.

24

Music Lessons

Lana and Nina watched Jeanie and the bartender walk away. When the former musician began to turn back to her husband, Lana asked, "Hey, Nina. Could I ask you an off-the-wall question about record companies and publishing rights?"

As much as Lana trusted Mitch to tell her the truth, he seemed too glib about the demise of his label. From what she could glean from Guy's article and the resulting follow-up pieces written by other reporters, LowDown Records' bankruptcy had meant the end of many bands, and those that survived had had to fight hard to do so. Especially since their royalties hadn't been paid in almost a year.

Nina stopped in her tracks and chuckled. "That's not what I was expecting you to ask. Sure, I'm all ears."

"If a record label goes bankrupt, is it difficult for the musicians to regain the rights to their songs?" To Lana, it seemed logical that the rights would automatically revert to the artists, but she was not a musician, and knew nothing about the music world.

Nina snorted. "Difficult? If their contract states that the label holds the copyrights, then it is pretty much impossible. Even major artists can't regain control over their master tapes—think about what happened to Taylor Swift after her record label was bought up by another."

Lana was flabbergasted. "But why? Shouldn't the songwriters control what happens to their work?"

"Why should they? Those master tapes are a label's most valuable asset, and the copyrights on those recordings are how they make their money. When a label is declared bankrupt, the tapes and copyrights are sold to pay off massive debts. What is really frustrating is that the master tapes and copyrights are usually sold to another label. Because the artist did not sign a contract with them, the new label does not owe them any royalties earned from those copyrights. I know quite a few musicians who gave up on music after that happened to them. They were too bitter and hurt to go on recording."

"Wait a second. After the new label buys the master tapes of previously released works, they do not owe the musicians any royalties?" Lana said, looking to Nina for confirmation.

"Precisely."

"Wow. That's pretty horrible. Do musicians have any sort of recourse when their label goes bankrupt?"

"There isn't a whole lot they can do, at least not to get their master tapes back. The only real option is to file a lawsuit claiming breach of contract against the defunct label, in the hopes of getting paid an estimation of what your future royalties would have been. But there are no guarantees that the courts will recognize the musician as a valid claimant, or that there will be enough money to actually get paid. If the courts do agree that they have a claim, then the musician becomes one of the many debtors the bankrupt estate owes money to and wouldn't receive any priority."

"That sounds like a raw deal."

Nina shrugged. "The music industry is really tough to break into, and even tougher to make money at. Producing and recording albums, at least through the traditional channels, can costs tens of thousands of dollars, and then you have to manufacture and market them, as well. I guess it's the same with books, movies, and theater productions—there are no guarantees that the investors will make their money back. The sad fact is, most do not."

"Thanks, that's good to know." Lana bit on her lip, taking in all Nina had told her. "And I take it starting up a label would be expensive, as well? Even if it was only to release your own music."

Nina bobbed and shook her head simultaneously. "It depends. If there are no live instruments, then it would be quite inexpensive to record everything yourself. However, if a band of musicians wanted to record an album, it would be trickier to set up. Most experienced musicians have enough gear to put together a decent mini-recording studio in their house. But it is not cheap."

Lana contemplated her words. "So you are saying that setting up an independent label and recording an album would require a fairly large investment?"

"Yes, you could say that. Why are you asking?"

Lana blushed. "Honestly, the questions about a label going bankrupt were inspired by your conversation with Mitch about LowDown Records. It made me curious, that's all, and I didn't want to ask Mitch about it. I had a feeling it might be too sensitive of a topic."

Nina nodded enthusiastically. "I feel you." The musician looked around the room until she spotted Mitch, still on the podium. "Word on the street is that there was more to the LowDown Records story than was reported on in the mainstream media."

"What do you mean?" Lana leaned in to better hear her.

"Apparently the reporter who broke the article had discovered that the feds were on to the embezzling scheme, too. The reporter tipped the label's owner off, and they struck a deal. The reporter waited to print it until after the label's owner had fled the country and was handsomely rewarded for it."

Lana's jaw about dropped to the floor. "Wait a second—are you saying that Guy Smith received money from LowDown Records' owner, and that thanks to Guy, he was able to flee the country? Yikes. I wonder if Mitch knows."

Nina's brow furrowed. "Did you say Guy Smith? Isn't that the reporter who got killed in the pub?"

"Yes, I did."

The musician's frown deepened. "That's a horrible coincidence. If I was Mitch, I would have happily have bashed that man over the head." Nina paled as she stammered, "I didn't mean that Mitch killed him, mind you."

"No, of course not," Lana soothed, wondering whether that was exactly what had happened.

25

Silver Lining

After her group's members were safely back in their hotel rooms, Lana stretched out on her bed and searched for the Anders Band on Spotify. When she found Mitch's newly released album, she turned the volume up and let the folksy music fill the room. It wasn't her preferred style, but the Irish-inspired melodies were danceable and upbeat. Even through her tinny speakers, it was apparent that the quality of the recording was superb, which probably meant that Mitch had spent quite a bit on the recording and production.

After the fifth song, Lana clicked on his name to see what else he had released. The music streaming service only linked back to Sampson & Anders.

"Are you kidding me?" she mumbled to the screen. Sampson & Anders had released ten albums, all with LowDown Records. She did a quick internet search and discovered the rights were now held by a small music label out of Colorado. Would either member of Sampson & Anders be receiving royalty checks? Based on all she'd read about the label's demise, only if they were the songwriters, she suspected. Seeing as not all the musicians in a band actually wrote the songs, Lana did a quick search to see who penned their music. Sure enough, Mitch's musical partner, George Sampson, had written all but a handful of their released songs.

Ten albums recorded and no royalties. How could Mitch be so casual about LowDown's deceit and demise, especially if he had no other source of income? Lana would have been raging mad about it. *Speaking of money,* she thought, *why did he come on this trip, if he is broke or close to it?*

Lana tried looking for factual confirmation that Guy had tipped the owner of LowDown Records off, but she couldn't find anything concrete in the mainstream media. There was a two-sentence reference to the rumor in a Seattle magazine's gossip column, and several mentions of it on Facebook and Twitter, but the story had not been picked up by any of the larger newspapers.

If Nina had heard about this story, would Mitch have? And even if Mitch had known about the tipoff, would he have held Guy accountable enough to have murdered him in cold blood? Or would his anger have been directed at the record label, instead?

There was only one way to find out. She looked at her clock and realized that her interrogation would have to wait; 1:00 a.m. was way too late to question one of her guests.

Yet Lana's mind didn't want to shut down quite yet. "Are you awake? Feel like chatting. Kiss, L," she messaged her boyfriend, Alex, not wanting to wake him up with a phone call in the middle of the night. He had stressed that this was going to be an intense and trying week, and she didn't want to interrupt his much-needed sleep or scare him into thinking something was wrong.

When her phone rang minutes later, Lana felt a surge of happiness. "Hey, Alex."

"It's Kitty," a female voice said, instead. "Are you expecting him to call? I can ring you back later."

"No, it's okay. I was more hoping than expecting it to be Alex. How are you holding up?"

Kitty laughed cynically. "Let's just say this is not the relaxing vacation that Jeremy and I were looking forward to."

Lana clicked her tongue in sympathy. "I wish there was something I could do to help."

"You are already doing so much for us. The lawyer's investigator is also on the case, but he is not having much luck finding another suspect or motive, and the police have no new leads. Guy's article was the clincher, it seems, and until they find someone with a stronger motive, I don't think Jeremy is going anywhere. But then, the police aren't privy to your group's conversations. Have you heard anything useful?"

Lana sighed. "Honestly, I'm not sure. I am certain that the O'Tooles had nothing to do with it. Nina, Paddy, and Patrick didn't know Guy, and their lives have not been destroyed or affected by an article he's written, either. Out of our group, three are potential suspects, but I wouldn't say that any of them had enough of a motive to actually kill him."

"Who has the strongest motive, of the three?" Kitty asked, her tone filled with exasperation. "And do you think one of them came here to Dublin to bump him off?"

"Devon's life has been ruined, thanks to Guy's lies, but I can't imagine him killing anyone—he just doesn't seem like a violent or aggressive person," Lana said. "And from what I can tell, he and his wife definitely did not want to run into Guy. Before he was killed, Evelyn had said something about how simply seeing Guy again might send Devon back into therapy."

"What about the other two?" Kitty pushed.

"Guy wrote an article about Mitch's label, LowDown Records, that set off a chain of events that ended with him losing the royalties to his songs."

"So Guy destroyed his life, too."

"In an indirect way. I don't know if Mitch blames Guy, specifically. He seems more upset with the record label's owner, which makes sense considering he was the one doing the embezzling. Though it looks like Guy tipped off the owner about a federal investigation into his illegal activities, which allowed him to flee the country before he could be arrested. It may also be that the owner paid Guy off for sharing the information with him."

"Wow, it sounds like Guy helped the label's owner to get away and also profited off of it. If I were Mitch, I would hold him responsible, as well as the record label's owner."

"I get what you mean, but Mitch did seem quite surprised to learn that it was Guy who wrote that article. But then again, he may have been lying to me."

"You mentioned a third suspect?"

Lana sighed heavily. "I know you like Jeanie, but she is unpredictable and lies so easily, it's tough to know if we can trust her or not. She is still a suspect in my book."

"What do you mean?"

"After denying it several times, she finally admitted that Guy was the former lover she was hoping to reunite with. The thing is, Jeanie hadn't actually told him she was coming over."

"And he rejected her as soon as he saw her. Ouch. But doesn't mean that she's a killer," Kitty finished with a sigh. "Look, I don't know Jeanie, either, but she was kind to me on the plane and seemed nice enough. For all I know, she was playing me the whole time," she said, her desperation spilling through the phone line. "But I do believe she came here out of love, not with the intention to hurt Guy."

Lana blew out her cheeks. "I'm afraid that is all I have."

"None of this is going to help Jeremy, is it?" Kitty snapped. "If it wasn't a stranger, then it must be one of them!"

"Three of our guests have a connection to Guy, and I'm keeping my ears open, but so far, I haven't found out anything suspicious or incriminating. I wish I could do more. But right now, I am at a total loss as to which one it might be."

"Oh, Lana, you're doing more than the police and our lawyer, put together! I'm sorry for getting cross with you. It all feels so hopeless right now. I cannot fathom having to fly back to Seattle without my husband, and then having to tell our three children that their daddy is locked up in a foreign land."

Lana had to fight back the tears as she envisioned Kitty's predicament. "Try to put it out of your mind. Somehow, we will find a way out of this. You have to believe it to be true, no matter how hopeless things seem right now."

"I'm trying, Lana, I really am. But I'm having real trouble finding the silver lining in this cloud."

26

Tracing Lineage

March 15—Day Four of the Wanderlust Tour in Dublin, Ireland

"Hey, Lana," Nina called out as she bounced into view. The rest of the group was spread out across the lobby, most still half-asleep. The itinerary was crammed full today, and to do it all, they had to get an early start.

"Our taxi is going to pick us up in a few minutes. Limerick is about two hours away, so we are going to make a day out of it."

"Great, thanks for letting us know," Lana answered. "Will you be back in time for dinner?"

Nina shook her head. "Paddy is hoping his cousins will invite us to eat with them and maybe even spend the night. Otherwise, we'll grab a bite in the village. With a little luck, we will run into someone local who can tell Paddy some old stories about their family," Nina said, wistfully. Her smile suddenly cracked.

"I sure hope they let us in. It has been two generations since anyone from the American side has been back, and contact has been, um, sporadic." Nina looked down as she finished.

Paddy sprinted over to his wife. "The cab's here, but Dad is still up in his room. He's changed his mind about joining us, he says, but he doesn't want to go with the tour group either. I'm not letting him sit in a pub and drink the day away. Could you help me get him downstairs?"

Nina rolled her eyes. "Why he insisted on coming to Ireland if he doesn't even want to see his family's home or village is beyond me. You would think he would be slightly curious to see where his father grew up. Alright, let's go get Pops." Nina waved to the rest. "See you tomorrow."

Before the O'Tooles returned downstairs, their bus to Glasnevin Cemetery arrived and her group piled in. On the ride over, everyone was quite subdued, and Lana swore she heard snoring. As much as she wanted to interrogate Mitch, she ultimately decided their short drive across the city center was not the right moment to do so. Besides, she was looking forward to seeing more of the local architecture, as well as crossing the River Liffey and the Royal Canal.

However, she didn't get the chance to check out the sights because Jeanie's latest shenanigans demanded her attention.

"Say, Evelyn, did you get my email with the link to leave a review?" Jeanie plopped down in the row in front of the couple as soon as the bus pulled away from the hotel.

Evelyn and Devon were sitting at the back, cuddling with their heads close together. Whatever Devon was murmuring in her ear, was making Evelyn blush. Jeanie's intrusion made them pull apart.

"I don't check email while I'm on vacation. I'll do it after we get back to Seattle, okay?"

Jeanie frowned. "It's better to do it while you're thinking about it. Tell you what," she said, pulling out her mobile, "why don't you fill it in now? You can use my phone."

Jeanie shoved it in Evelyn's face as everyone in the group turned to stare at her.

Lana's jaw just about hit the floor. "Ah, Jeanie, if Evelyn doesn't want to post a review right now, maybe you should let her enjoy the trip. There's no rush, right?"

She knew from experience how important online reviews were, but Jeanie's insistence that she write a review of her genealogy services was grating on Lana's nerves, and she could only imagine how Evelyn was feeling.

"If Ev doesn't want to write a review right now, then she doesn't have to.

You've sent your request via email; why don't you let it rest?" Devon said.

Jeanie clicked her tongue. "What do you know about running your own business? Do you have any idea how difficult it is to survive in the competitive world of genealogical research? I need every review I can get."

Her remark about being self-employed seemed to temper Devon's attitude. Evelyn apparently noticed how her husband had drawn into himself, because she grabbed Jeanie's phone and ticked in a few words before returning it.

"There. Now we can all move on."

Jeanie scrolled up to see what Evelyn had written, her satisfied smile freezing as she read the text.

"'Reasonable results for the money spent, three stars,'" she read aloud. "Hmm, it doesn't have the pizzazz or rating I was hoping for, but it is appreciated." She snapped her phone shut and moved to the front of the bus without another word.

Not even a thank you, Lana thought, amazed by Jeanie's audacity. *If I was Evelyn, I would have given her one star.*

She didn't have time to worry about Jeanie or Evelyn because their bus began to slow, signaling their imminent arrival at their destination. As they rolled towards the Glasnevin Cemetery parking lot, Lana stared out the window, taking in the high walls, ancient evergreens, and skinny watch towers dotting the complex. Not only was it one of the most important places in Ireland for genealogical research, it was also significant for cultural-historic reasons. Built in the 1830s, it was the final resting place of over one-and-a-half million souls, including many important politicians, poets, playwrights, novelists, and musicians.

"Do you see those seven towers surrounding the graveyard?" she called out to her group.

Her clients murmured in the affirmative as they twisted in their seats to better see them.

"They used to be manned by armed guards because the graves here were a favorite target for body snatchers!"

"Oooh! I hope they didn't steal any of my relatives," Jeanie joked.

After their taxi driver dropped them off, Randy and Lana navigated their group through the dense crowds towards the entrance to the gravesites. The many visitors crammed onto the winding paths attested to the fact that it was one of Ireland's most popular tourist attractions. They followed the flow of pedestrian traffic past the café, gift shop, and flower stands towards the visitor center.

When she saw the size of the place, Lana was immediately glad that they had been able to take part in an organized tour. The cemetery was a series of sprawling plots of land joined together by paths. Each appeared to be chock-full of graves, meaning it would probably take them hours to walk through it all. Without a guide to point out the more interesting tombstones, they probably would have wandered around aimlessly and not have learned much about the place or its permanent residents.

When they passed a funky curved building made primarily of glass, Evelyn exclaimed, "That's where the Genealogy Research Service is located! They are going to send me all of their results via email, but I would like to stop by and talk with the archivists before we leave."

"You mentioned that before. We should have time after the Dead Interesting Tour to visit the center," Lana confirmed. "Jeanie wants to talk to the archivists, as well. Don't you, Jeanie?"

"Yes, I do. I have scoured their online archives but am also hoping they can find a few older records that may point me in the right direction."

They quickly found their guide and joined a group of forty others. For the next hour, they dutifully followed him around as he led them in a crisscross pattern over the vast terrain. The graves were crammed together but seemed to be extremely well-cared for. There were several mausoleum-style crypts, but most of the plots were topped by Celtic crosses or statues of weeping angels, saints, or statesmen. The deep emerald of the tall evergreen trees surrounding much of the property provided a lovely contrast to the sea of beige and gray stones. Lana particularly enjoyed seeing the French-Irish war memorial, featuring a Celtic cross and a helmet decorated with a shamrock.

They strolled casually along the paths, enjoying the Victorian gardens as they learned more about the fascinating and famous Irish men and women buried here. The tour was as much as a lesson in Irish history as it was a performance piece. At several graves, actresses and actors read from the deceased's written works or recited their famous speeches. It was a vastly entertaining and educational visit.

Most of her group stayed with the rest, but Lana was continually having to shoo Jeanie along. Her insistence at lingering in the graveyard and reading the tombstones was, to Lana, a touch morbid. At least, that was how it felt until Jeanie called over to Evelyn, "I bet some of these are my distant relatives. Maybe yours, too."

No wonder Jeanie is so interested—she is certain her family is in amongst the dead, Lana thought. Being surrounded by all this history reminded her of the O'Tooles, currently on their way to Patrick's ancestral home. She hoped the experience was everything Paddy hoped it would be.

Just before their guide wrapped up his spiel, he tapped on his microphone, getting their undivided attention again.

"Before I go, here are your passes for a free consultation in our genealogical archives. If you fancy knowing if you've got Irish blood running through your veins, I would stop by."

He handed a small card to each guest before tipping his hat to them and scurrying back to the visitor center.

"What did you think?" Lana asked after her clients had regrouped.

"This is the most fascinating tour I have ever been on!" Jeanie enthused. "I cannot believe how many famous people are buried here. Hopefully the archives will be able to help me figure out which ones are my ancestors."

"Do we have time to walk around on our own?" Mitch asked. "There was a tombstone I would like to get a picture of before we leave."

Lana nodded. "Sure, okay. We have about an hour before our bus meets us by the entrance. Does anyone else want to walk around the graveyard?"

"I would rather visit the archives now," Evelyn said. "This will be my only chance to talk to them face to face, and I want to make the most of it."

"If we have time afterwards, maybe we can walk through the Experience Glasnevin museum, but I've seen enough headstones for one tour," Devon added.

"How exciting," Jeanie cooed. "I hope they were able to locate some new information in their older archives. From the papers you showed me, I was able to find out quite a bit for your mother. You do know that all of their digitalized files are accessible through the databases that I have subscriptions to, don't you? It might be that I already found all there is to find. I would hate for you to get your hopes up."

Evelyn cocked her head. "No, I did not. But that is good to know. I will have to subscribe to a few of the genealogy databases, as well."

Jeanie's eyes narrowed. "True, you don't have to be a professional researcher to subscribe. I usually don't recommend that amateurs attempt it—there are so many variables that have to be just right when you are searching through those databases. If you follow the wrong name, you may end up wasting months searching in the wrong records."

"I spent twenty-seven years of my life researching the histories of centuries-old cultural objects for some of the most prestigious museums in the United States. I think I'll be fine." Evelyn practically spat the words at her. She grabbed her husband's arm and walked off in the direction of the research center, leaving Jeanie gaping after them.

Randy's eyebrows shot up before he looked to Lana and shrugged.

"Jeanie, what do you want to do now?"

She turned to Lana and smiled as if nothing strange had just happened. "I could use a bite to eat before I visit with the archivists."

"I would love to have a snack—if you don't mind the company," Randy said.

Jeanie half curtsied. "It would be an honor to dine with you."

"Great! I am happy to keep you company, Mitch," Lana said, already thinking of how she could ask him about LowDown Records and his royalties.

"Sure, as long as you don't mind taking a picture of me with one of my heroes," Mitch said with a smile.

27

Dubliner

The large white tombstone before her was almost as high as Lana was tall. Carved into the surface in large letters were three words: "LUKE KELLY, Dubliner." Mitch stood at the foot end, his head bowed.

"Who is Luke Kelly?" Lana asked, after giving him a few minutes alone to talk with the deceased.

"The singer for The Dubliners—possibly the greatest band Ireland has ever produced. Trust me, if you had ever heard him sing, you would recognize Luke Kelly's voice in a heartbeat. He breathed new life and soul into many classic Irish songs." Mitch gazed down at his hero's final resting place. "I have learned so much by studying The Dubliners' music."

Lana studied the simple stone. "He died young."

"He had a brain tumor and struggled with alcoholism. He was only forty-three when he passed, but he left a musical legacy to rival the most prolific of musicians."

"I'll have to listen to his work later."

"Do. You won't regret it." Mitch pulled out his phone and handed it to Lana. "Could you take a few pictures of me with his headstone?"

"Naturally." After Lana took several snaps of him posing with his arm over the tombstone and then squatting next to the grave, they turned back to the visitor center. Mitch seemed content to walk in silence, but Lana couldn't let this opportunity go to waste.

"Say, did you get the rights back to your songs after LowDown went under?"

He tensed up visibly but kept his eyes on the path before them. "No. Some of us filed a lawsuit to get our master tapes back, but LowDown's trustees hired better lawyers, and all we did is waste the rest of our savings. The master recordings were ultimately sold off to different record companies."

Which means he is not receiving royalties on them, Lana recalled.

"Why do you ask?"

"Our talk about LowDown Records reminded me of an article I had read in a Seattle music magazine about the embezzlement investigation," she explained. "It was something about how the label's owner paid Guy Smith to hold the publication of that article until he had left the country. Do you know which one I mean?"

Mitch turned to her, glowering with rage. "Of course I do. But it wasn't just local gossip—a few of the other musicians on the label had heard the same thing from different sources and were posting about it on their social media. Why the story was never picked up by the mainstream media is beyond me."

"You said you were glad that Guy wrote that article about LowDown Records, but in fact, its publication gave the owner time to flee the country before he could be taken in for questioning by the FBI. And from what I could find online, it sounds like he had several weeks to prepare his departure. Which meant he was also able to funnel most of the record label's profits abroad before the IRS could freeze the accounts. None of you were compensated for your missing royalties, were you?"

"No," Mitch hissed. "That vermin managed to get to Vanuatu before the article hit the newsstands. The government seemed completely blindsided, both that he had escaped and that he had taken the money with him. LowDown represented more musicians than all of the other local labels combined. Since he had not paid out any royalties in almost a year, it would have been millions that he stole from us. Seeing as he's living in a country that doesn't extradite to the US, I doubt any of us will ever see a dime. I hated Guy for that."

"You told the police you didn't know who Guy was. Why did you lie—did you kill him?"

He looked her straight in the eye. "I would have happily strangled him with my bare hands, given the chance. But I didn't. I'm sorry about your friend, but I'm not the killer."

"If you weren't here because of Guy, why are you in Dublin then?" Lana pushed. "And how can you afford the trip?"

"If you must know, I am here to find work. Your boss, Dotty Thompson, is a fan of my music and gave me a significant discount on this trip. My solo album is more Irish influenced than the Sampson & Anders material was—that is why I've been playing at as many pubs as possible so I can build up a network. And it's working. I already have ten gigs lined up for this summer and a few leads on festivals I may be able to play at."

"That's wonderful, Mitch! I'm glad to hear it's working out for you."

He smiled shyly. "Me, too. I honestly wasn't certain it would. The whole LowDown debacle shook my confidence in the music industry to the core. But I am my own boss now and in a much better place for it."

He looked down the tree-lined path, teeming with visitors snapping pictures of everything in sight. "If you don't have any more questions, shall we rejoin the rest?"

28

The Wrong Riley

By the time Lana and Mitch got back to the bus, the rest of the group was already standing next to it. As they approached, Lana couldn't help but notice how Evelyn was scowling at the genealogist. *What did Jeanie do now? That woman is nothing but drama*, she thought.

"How could you?" Evelyn hissed.

Jeanie brushed an invisible piece of lint off of her jacket, but did not make eye contact. "What do you mean?"

Evelyn held up a pile of papers. "You charged my mother-in-law hundreds of dollars for search results that she could have gotten for free."

Jeanie sucked in her breath, but said nothing.

Evelyn threw her hands up in the air and turned to walk away from the bus. Worried her client might not want to stay on the tour, Lana sprung in front of her.

"What do you mean, Evelyn?"

She looked to the paperwork in her hand, now trembling violently. "I sent the information my mother-in-law had already collected to the cemetery's archivist, so she could use it as a starting point. Almost all of the information Jeanie had found came from their digitalized records, which are accessible for free online. In my book, Devon's mom shouldn't have had to pay for it."

Jeanie threw her hands on her hips. "Then she should have done the research herself, instead of hiring me to do it for her! My work methods are clearly listed on my website. Your mother-in-law chose to hire me; I didn't force her to sign the contract engaging my services."

"All you did is copy and paste information you found in freely accessible archives! What about all those expensive subscription services you use?" Evelyn pressed. Lana had never seen her so riled up.

"I always use several databases to create a far more complete picture than only one can. It has been months since I worked on your mother's family tree, but I am certain I cross-referenced all of them. However, I cannot guarantee that I will find a lead in each one. And to be clear, clients pay for my database access, as well as my extensive knowledge of the craft. Even you have to admit that I found enough to put you on the right path."

"The right path? For what my mother-in-law paid you, I expected the whole family tree, not a few branches and twigs."

"Give me a break," Jeanie countered. "Did you really expect me to contact every archive in Ireland for that price? The long-distance calls and postage alone would have cost more than your mother-in-law paid me. No, clients pay for access to the genealogy databases that I subscribe to, but I don't follow paper trails. It is stated quite clearly on my website."

"Does your price include the fabrications, or do you throw those in for free?"

Jeanie froze as Evelyn shoved a sheet of paper in her face. "The archivist was glad I had stopped by because there were two glaring discrepancies in the research report I had given her. One of the names listed on the family tree was the wrong spelling of Riley. You mixed up two surnames and traced the wrong Riley back to Cork, when you should have been looking in Galway, meaning that whole branch is useless. And here I thought that mixing up the names was an amateur mistake," Evelyn needled.

Jeanie's cheeks were as red as a ripe tomato. When she opened her mouth to respond, Evelyn rushed to add, "And another name appears to be a complete fabrication. There was a gap in the online archives that they were able to fill in with their older, paper archive registers, the ones that had not yet been digitalized. Yet you had filled in a name, one they cannot match to any record in their archives. It appears to be made up."

Jeanie grew even redder as Evelyn continued her tirade. "The archivists warned me that this was a trick by some genealogical researchers—to fill in the gaps so their clients felt as if they were getting their money's worth."

"How dare you talk to me like that?" Jeanie jabbed Evelyn in the chest. "That is a pretty hefty accusation—are you certain you can back up that claim?"

Randy stepped in between the two women. "Enough. Let's get on the bus so we don't miss our next tour. Why don't you two get on first." He nodded to the Rileys, then looked to Jeanie. "Could you please sit towards the back?"

"What a waste of money," Evelyn huffed as she rushed past Jeanie and stepped onto the bus.

"If it's such a waste, why do I have a waiting list for clients wanting my help tracing their family's histories?" Jeanie shrieked and began to follow. Lana sprung in front of her and waved the other guests onboard.

Yet Evelyn was unwilling to let their argument go so easily. "Do you lie to all of your clients, or is my mother-in-law special?" she shouted over the bus seats, pointing her finger menacingly at Jeanie. Her eyes were bulging out of their sockets. She was getting so upset it was almost scary.

"Darling, don't let her get to you," Devon soothed. "She's not worth it. You're going to take over Mom's research now, anyway, so you don't have to worry about scammers like her anymore."

"Did you just call me a scammer?" Jeanie screamed. "I have had enough of your insults! I am a qualified researcher who has made hundreds of families happy with my findings. And you might find my prices high, but I assure you, they are quite reasonable."

Jeanie plopped down onto a seat at the front and threw her arms over her torso, her facial expression daring anyone else to question her rates or work methods.

After the bus pulled into traffic, Lana darted back to Randy.

He leaned in close and said, "If they can't resolve their differences, this is going to be a long three days."

"Luckily, the tour is already over the halfway point, but I know what you mean. Let me see if I can get Jeanie to back down," Lana said.

"Good luck with that," Randy whispered. "I'll see how the Rileys are feeling, but I suspect I already know the answer."

Unfortunately, this was not the first time they'd had to separate bickering clients, and both knew the best way to deal with the situation was to keep them as far away from each other as possible so they could cool off. After they had done that, then it was time for the guides to check each client's mood and see whether there was room for compromise. There usually was not, especially directly after the confrontation. Still, they both knew it was worth a shot.

She squeezed Randy's shoulder and slipped in next to Jeanie.

29

Stay or Go

Lana looked to her client, who steadfastly gazed out at the traffic. Jeanie was not going to give in easily, that was certain. She saw no other choice but to be extremely blunt. "Are you going to give Devon's mother a refund?"

"Why should I? My rates are posted on my website, as are my research methods—I didn't cheat her out of anything. I did exactly what she wanted and charged her accordingly."

"Did you really just copy and paste what you had found in the cemetery's freely accessible digital archives?"

"People are too lazy to do the research themselves, so I can charge what I want for the results I find. I'm certain that I checked the other archives—I cross-reference them all for each research assignment—but they must not have included references to the right Rileys. If Evelyn had not come here, she never would have known. She can only be mad at herself for not having done the work," Jeanie maintained.

"So how did the wrong Riley end up in the family tree?"

"Do you know how many Irish surnames have changed over the years? New variations develop and catch on, and before you know it, Ó Raghailligh could also be O'Reilly, Rilley with two *l*'s, Riley with one *l*... I think you get my drift. So I chose the wrong Riley. Naming inconsistencies have confounded many a genealogist, so it's no reflection on me or my services."

"Why did you make up a relative?" Lana pressed.

"I didn't make anyone up!" Jeanie hissed. "It must have been a transcription error. But it was certainly not intentional."

"Don't people pay you to get your research right? At some point, someone is going to catch on."

Jeanie's eyebrows shot up. "What are you insinuating?"

Lana wondered whether Jeanie truly did not understand what she was saying, or whether she was simply unwilling to admit that she had lied to a client. "It sounds like you are picking a random name and trying to pass it off as the correct one. You do understand that Evelyn sees this as a form of fraud, right? And I tend to agree."

"What is with you two—it's not fraud! I did my job. I don't know if you have ever done any genealogical research, but it's not as easy as putting a name into a database. Ireland is especially tough because the vast majority of its nineteenth-century census records were destroyed in a fire at the Public Records Office of Ireland in 1922. Only fragments survive. To matters more difficult, births and marriages were not registered before 1864. To fill in a family's entire tree, a researcher would most likely have to examine a slew of paper records held in local parishes and cemeteries. Not all of them are digitized yet, and a flight from Seattle to Dublin is not cheap. People pay me to search databases, not to take a trip. And they expect results, not to hear that I could not find a thing."

"Wait, are you admitting that you may have made up a name or two over the years?"

Jeanie whipped her head away. "Most of my clients are extremely satisfied with their results; that's all I care about."

Am I crazy or is Jeanie a swindler? Lana stared at the back of her client's head, wondering how many other customers she had faked names or dates for. It almost sounded as if lies and deceit were part of her business model.

Another thought took hold as her client steadfastly refused to turn around. If Jeanie truly did not understand the moral difference between right and wrong, could she have killed Guy when he rejected her? That possibility sure seemed more plausible now than it had a few hours ago.

Whether or not she was a killer, it was clear that Jeanie was not about to admit that she lied to Evelyn. One look at the Rileys made clear that the couple were not going to forgive and forget, either. Even Randy's puppy dog eyes were not able to break their evil glare, still focused on Jeanie.

"I don't know if having you remain on this tour is a good idea," she said, wondering what Jeanie's response was going to be.

"Why should I leave? I did nothing wrong. If Evelyn is uncomfortable, then she can go home. I paid top dollar to see Dublin, and I expect to get every penny's worth."

"Let me talk to Randy about how we are going to move forward, but if you all stay, I think it is better if we separate you two as much as possible."

"I don't care what you do, so long as I get to see everything on our itinerary." Jeanie wrapped her arms back around her torso and turned so her gaze was focused out the window.

Case closed, Lana thought as she looked back to Randy and shrugged. "We did our best," he mouthed back at her.

30

Family Ties

After a tense bus ride to their next stop, Lana was hoping her guests would be so interested in the sights that they would let their feud go. Unfortunately, nothing could have been further from the truth.

As soon as they descended into the crypts of Saint Michan and saw the mummified bodies the church was famous for, Jeanie vomited all over Evelyn and Devon's shoes. Her refusal to refund their genealogical research or pay for new footwear meant that Lana and Randy had to double their efforts at keeping the peace.

After a short detour back to the hotel to let the Rileys change their shoes and Jeanie her dress, Lana and Randy got their guests to Dublin Castle in time for their next excursion. All of them were impressed by the grand staircases, the many magnificent paintings, and the opulent rooms decorated with gold and lit by impressive chandeliers.

Too soon, they were rushing to a riverboat for a short cruise along the River Liffey. The contemporary architecture lining its banks that Lana found rather drab during the daytime came to life in the evening. Most were outlined with colorful strips of light that she found charming. The majority were colored green, as homage to the Saint Patrick's Day celebration in two days' time. The riverboat cruise was also the perfect way to see the many bridges Dublin was known for. Lana's favorite was the gorgeous harp-shaped bridge named after playwright and novelist Samuel Beckett.

By the time they got their guests back to the hotel that evening, they were all exhausted.

"It's a free night, folks. If you want a list of restaurant suggestions, just let me or Randy know, and we can reserve a table for you. There are also plenty of tours you can take, all of which are listed on our optional excursions page."

"I reserved a place on the Hellfire Club tour," Jeanie said.

"Oh, yes, that does sound like a fun one," Lana said. She had read about the haunted hunting lodge up on Mount Pelier Hill, mostly known as a place that devil worshippers and dabblers in black magic used to celebrate nights of debauchery back in the mid-1700s. The Supernatural Dublin Tour Jeanie had booked was supposed to be quite a kick.

Lana checked her list of reservations. Indeed, Jeanie was booked on it, as were Jeremy and Kitty. Seeing her friends' names on the itinerary list brought a tear to her eye.

"We have dinner reservations but could use a taxi," Devon piped up.

"Are you sure? I was hoping we could walk. It's only a few blocks away, and the rain has finally subsided," Evelyn countered.

Devon pulled her close. "That is a great point. We won't need the taxi after all, Lana."

The two strolled out of the hotel, arm in arm. Lana was glad to see them getting along so well. This trip really did seem to be saving their marriage. Though Guy's death may have had something to do with their improved moods, she considered.

"I think you all know where I want to go," Mitch said with a laugh. "I'm going to get my guitar and head out. Have a good night, everyone."

Everybody is sorted so now I have a little time for myself, Lana thought. She dialed her boyfriend's number as soon as she was inside her hotel room, but Alex did not pick up.

"Where the heck is he?" she muttered. Lana fought back a wave of annoyance as she reminded herself that he had made quite clear that he was going to be too busy to talk to her this week.

Feeling restless and a little hungry, Lana pulled her rain jacket back on and headed downstairs to hit the streets and find a snack.

However, catching sight of Patrick at the hotel's bar made Lana deviate from her path. Given their long drive, she had half-expected the O'Tooles to spend the night with their newfound relatives, not already be back at the hotel.

"How was the trip?" Lana asked.

"It's a gas station," Patrick said, then began laughing so hard that she was worried he was going to fall off the barstool.

"What is a gas station?"

"Granddad's house! Isn't that hilarious?" he roared. "No, wait—it's a gas!" His guffaw filled the bar.

A surge of irritation washed over Lana. Paddy and Nina were two of the nicest guests she had led on a tour, and Patrick's constant negativity was grating, to say the least. Her frustration with not being able to reach Alex and with Patrick's attitude boiled over. "Do you hate Ireland or your son?"

Her remark shut his joy right down. "What? I don't hate my son, and I don't know enough about Ireland to judge it yet. From what Dad had told me, I had expected more rain, worse beer, and fewer interesting places to visit."

"Then why are you so against Paddy seeing his ancestral home?"

"Ancestral on paper maybe," Patrick huffed. "I don't consider myself Irish, and I don't understand the fuss Paddy is making about his roots. My dad was Irish, not me—and certainly not my son. And if Dad didn't want to visit, why should Paddy or I?"

"But your son did want to see the house and had set his hopes on meeting the Irish side of his family. Why can't you support him in that?"

Patrick Senior locked eyes with Lana. "You don't understand. I would do anything to protect my boy. That's what family does, protect those they love. Maybe I've been going about it the wrong way…" His voice trailed off as he stared off into the distance.

Lana couldn't believe what she was hearing. "Protect him? I would not have used that word. You have made it quite clear that you think his desire to meet his family is a joke."

"No, that's not true. Paddy's insistence that it matters is the joke."

Lana plopped down on the barstool next to him. "You've lost me."

"If Paddy had just wanted to see the house or village, I would have wished him and Nina a safe journey and not said anything else about it. His interest in his Irish ancestors started out innocently enough, but after Dad died and he got ahold of his paperwork, things changed. I guess it was because the old pictures and documents made our Irish ancestry tangible. As soon as he saw that address, he could not stop talking about wanting to meet his family. And after he figured out how large the property was, it turned into an obsession! Suddenly, he's talking as if he's an Irish lord of some sort, which made me nervous. They might have had land, but they had a lot of kids to share it amongst. Dad was one of twelve, and I bet all of his brothers and sisters had large families, too. I doubt they were looking for an American relative to push his way into the mix and would have met him with suspicion, not open arms."

Lana glared at him. "Maybe they would have welcomed him into the fold, no questions asked. Why did you have to interfere?"

Patrick pounded his beer onto the bar. "I have a shoebox full of letters telling me otherwise!"

Her blank stare prompted him to explain.

"Names and dates on a piece of paper don't tell you what the person was like. My father left Limerick because his parents kicked him out! He never did have a good word to say about Ireland or his family. And I can't say I blame him—the only letters we have ever gotten from the old country were ones asking for money." When he turned to take a swig of his beer, Lana swore she saw him blink away a tear.

"I'm incredibly sorry to hear that." She touched his arm lightly, then pulled her hand away. It was the first time Patrick had shown any sign of emotion other than irritation since the trip began, and she was not entirely certain how to react.

He shrugged. "It is what it is. Some families would do anything for their members, but a lot of folks couldn't give two hoots about their relatives. I guess it's the luck of the draw. I do know you can't change the past or make someone want to get to know you better."

Lana shook her head slightly, wondering whether Patrick had always been so cynical. When he took a long swig of his beer, she shifted uncomfortably on the barstool, unsure what she should do.

When she started to rise, he said, "To be clear, I don't have any problem with people wanting to know more about their past. I get that they like knowing who their ancestors were because it makes them feel connected to a certain culture or country—and there's no harm in that. But my dad always said that it didn't matter where you came from—it's what you do now that counts. And I think he's right. That Jeanie lady keeps going on about her famous ancestors." He snorted. "Just because your great-great-great-granddaddy might have been royalty does not mean I have to treat you as such."

"Why did you come on this trip if you were so against Paddy meeting your Irish family?"

"To catch him when it all went wrong. Nina's a great girl, but she doesn't seem to understand what she is dealing with. In some ways, she's been encouraging him to get in touch with them, even after I showed her the letters asking for a handout. But you know what, I am glad that we all came over. It solved a mystery I had been trying to crack for quite a while."

"And that is?" Lana asked when Patrick fell silent.

"The last letter we got from them, begging for money, was dated two years ago. We found out today that they sold their land to the gas station a few months after they had sent it. Apparently, they made a fortune off of the deal, which must be why the letters stopped—they didn't need Dad's help anymore. If they had been interested in being a part of our lives, they would have stayed in touch. I'm glad Paddy didn't get caught up in all that bull honkey. He deserves better than that."

Lana looked at Patrick with new eyes. She never would have guessed his gruff remarks and veiled insults were actually made out of love for his son. "You are a really good dad, Patrick."

"I don't know about that," he muttered. "I just hope that Paddy wants to talk to me tomorrow. He's pretty cut up about not finding any kin in Limerick."

Lana looked around the bar. "Say, where are Paddy and Nina?"

"They went to bed. Paddy was so disappointed with how things went; I don't think he'll be joining us tomorrow. But we'll see. Maybe a good night's sleep will put some sense in him."

"Sleep sounds like a good idea. Are you going to stay up a while longer?"

Patrick raised his glass. "After I finish this, I'll be heading up to my room. Sleep well, Lana."

"You, too."

As she started to walk away, he called after her, "Do the police still have your friend in custody?"

"Yes, they do, I'm afraid. But I know he couldn't have done it."

"I am sorry to hear that—he and his wife seem like good people. If you want my two cents, the murder doesn't feel planned to me. More like someone saw their chance to bump off that reporter and took it. I wouldn't be surprised if it was a crime of passion, which means a female was probably involved. Women are always so dramatic."

31

Kisses and Wishes in Blarney

March 16—Day Five of the Wanderlust Tour in Dublin, Ireland

"They don't clean it, you know! Millions of people have kissed that thing. Think about your health!"

Lana's stomach sank as Jeanie's voice boomed down the steep staircase leading to one of Ireland's most treasured objects—the Blarney Stone. She double-timed it up the stairs, apologizing as she scooted around an older couple in her desire to reach her client before the castle's staff heard her scaring off would-be visitors.

She and Randy had split them into two groups, in order to keep Jeanie away from the Rileys. Neither the genealogist or the couple were willing to let their disagreement go, and it was the guides' job to do everything within their power to keep the group spirit positive and the tour conflict-free. Lana had taken the Rileys and O'Tooles with her, leaving Mitch and Jeanie with Randy.

Her group had started with a walk around the exterior, taking in the differences in height and building techniques of the partially ruined structures. The intention was to give Randy's group a forty-five-minute head start, but her group sped around the castle, uninterested in the crumbling walls or phenomenal views of the surrounding countryside. All they really wanted to do was see the stone and then explore the extensive garden—known for its witches, fairies, and wishing steps. *Can't get much more Irish than Blarney,* Lana thought when she spotted shamrocks in the grass. It had been tempting to stop and look for a four-leaf clover, but her group had kept walking towards the stone.

"I read that locals urinate on it!" Jeanie shrieked, bringing Lana back to the here and now.

Where is Randy? she wondered. Jeanie must have torn down the stairs without telling him where she was going. She still couldn't see her client or the top of the staircase from her current position.

"That's not true!" Lana yelled at the top of her lungs when several people waiting in line gasped and began retreating down the stairs. "It is a silly rumor, but physically impossible. The Blarney Stone is guarded by attendants during opening hours and a state-of-the-art security system at night. Besides, the stone itself is set into the rampart, at the base of a wall hanging several stories in the air," she reasoned. "You would have to break the laws of gravity to do so."

Her calm voice and reasonable explanation caused those who had turned around to stop and consider her words before ultimately ascending again. Lana had also seen blog posts about the persistent rumors and knew exactly what Jeanie was talking about. However, in contrast to her client, Lana had also read the reasons as to why it could not be—and was not—true.

"Can you please keep your opinions to yourself for a few minutes?" Randy chastised loudly, to Lana's relief. "These people have paid good money to be here. It's not their fault that you are claustrophobic."

"It is a disease—not a choice. I just can't handle being in small spaces," Jeanie wailed, her frustration audible even from a distance. Lana couldn't tell how far up the tower staircase Randy and Jeanie were because she still could not see either one of them.

"Of course not," Randy soothed. "But could you keep your voice down, at least until we get back outside?"

Jeanie hmphed loudly, but did refrain from speaking. At least until the two groups met on the staircase.

"Oh, Lana, it's good that I caught you," Jeanie cried. She grabbed Lana's arm tight. "Be aware of that rock—it's not clean!"

"Thanks, Jeanie. I am aware."

Sketchy hygiene or not, she wanted to see the stone, set high up in a tower above Blarney Castle. Whether she would actually kiss it remained to be seen.

"Hey, Lana," Randy said. "Mitch is still in line and should be close to the top of the rampart by now. He is going to meet Jeanie and me in the castle's café after he's kissed the stone."

"Sounds good, thanks for letting me know. We are going to be here a while, I imagine," she said, recalling the sign stating that it was a ninety-minute wait from the bottom of the staircase to the stone. "Should I call you when we are finished here?"

"Take your time; we still have to walk around the outside of the castle after Mitch is done."

"Okay, great. See you later," Lana replied as she moved up two more steps. At this rate, she wondered if the ninety-minute estimate was optimistic.

When Jeanie began moaning about how the walls were caving in on her, Randy took her by the elbow and propelled her down the steep flight of stairs. Jeanie was so self-absorbed, she hadn't even noticed the others.

What a drama queen, Lana thought while Jeanie carried on as if she was on her deathbed. Was Patrick right about it being a crime of passion, mostly likely committed by a woman? Jeanie was a liar and fraud—could she also be a killer? The older man did make a great point, but Lana couldn't believe it was Jeanie. Her client did have a motive for harming Guy, but she was so narcissistic that Lana doubted his rejection really bothered her that much. Since the tour began, Jeanie had hit on pretty much every male they had encountered. To Lana, she seemed more obsessed with the idea of being in love than with one particular person.

Who else could have killed Guy? She refused to believe it was Devon, but she also trusted Mitch when he said he hadn't gotten the chance to harm him.

"Why do people kiss the rock, anyway?" Nina asked, breaking Lana's train of thought.

"If you do, you will be granted seven years of eloquence." Lana was glad she and Paddy had joined them today. So far, neither one of them had breathed a word about their trip to Limerick, so Lana had to assume that Patrick's version of events was the truth.

"You mean the gift of gab?" Paddy asked. "Then Nina doesn't need to kiss the Blarney Stone—she was born with that."

"Hey!" She slapped his chest before they both broke out in laughter. "I guess I can't really get mad—you are right."

Paddy pulled her in close and kissed her cheek as Patrick looked on from a lower step, a smile on his face.

"I'm glad you two wanted to come today," the older man said softly. "I was worried about you, Paddy."

His son looked down at him. "I hate to say it, but you were right. I guess they were just out for money, but it would have been nice to have met at least a few of our Irish relatives while we were here."

Patrick nodded slowly. "I am sorry it didn't work out the way you hoped. But I am not sorry that you asked me to come along. Ireland is a beautiful country, and I'm glad we got to see it together," he said, his words bringing tears to his son's eyes as he reached out to his father.

Nina was also blinking back a few, Lana noted, as she watched her husband and father-in-law embrace.

Patrick Senior cleared his throat and looked to the side. "We haven't spent enough time together these past few years. It's my fault—I felt worthless after they let me go and took it out on those I loved. I only wish your mother had gotten this chance to see Ireland with us."

"It's good to get to know you again, Dad. And seeing as you are an Irish relative, I guess I got what I wished for," Paddy said.

Patrick laughed and slapped his son on the back. "You are absolutely right."

Paddy looked up at the line slowly winding its way around the tower. "Should we skip the stone and grab a Guinness?"

Patrick laid a hand on his son's shoulder. "I knew I raised you right."

Nina looked on, glowing with happiness. When they began to descend, she whispered in Lana's ear, "It worked!" then skipped after them.

Lana choked back a wave of emotion, thrilled to see the trip had brought father and son closer together. Suddenly, she realized her other clients were still in line.

"You two want to kiss the Blarney Stone, right?" Lana asked the Rileys.

"Definitely. It's worth the wait," Devon answered for them both.

"Excellent."

As they climbed higher up the tall tower made of stone, Lana understood why Jeanie was so freaked out. The staircase was extremely narrow; the ancient steps, uneven. She knew these old castle staircases were so slender and spiraling because it allowed for a better defense. But she still felt as if one misstep could mean tumbling backwards to her death. It didn't help that the higher they climbed, the closer the visitors crowded together, all eager to get out of the stairwell and back into the light.

When they finally wound their way out onto a small rampart, Lana's stomach about dropped when she saw how high up they were and where the stone was located. It was indeed embedded underneath a section of the outer wall. To kiss it, one had to hang over an opening in the tower and lean backwards. The drop alone made her about lose her nerve.

When it was her turn, she gulped as the guide helped her down onto a thick rug placed over the cold stone floor. She lay on her back and scooched out, holding onto the two rails for dear life, thankful for the safety bars underneath.

As she stretched her neck back, she saw the stone above her. Moments before she touched her lips to it, she wondered whether eloquence was worth risking contracting a weird disease. In that split second, she decided it was not and fake smooched the stone before allowing the attendant to help her back up. She was eloquent enough as it was.

After Devon, and Evelyn had kissed the stone, they picked up the O'Tooles from the bar and set off to explore the sixty acres of gardens surrounding the castle. They followed the trail leading to Rock Close—home to the Fairy Glade, Witch's Kitchen, Fern Garden, and Druid's Cave.

Lana was born and raised in the Pacific Northwest, so she was used to hiking through old-growth forests, but this was something out of a fairy tale.

Everywhere she looked there were blankets of moss and ivy covering rocks, paths, and tree trunks. It was magical. Seeing this, she understood why the attendants warned them to be on the lookout for leprechauns and fairies. Her group wandered along the path, oohing and aahing at the glorious ferns, waterfalls, rock formations, and ancient trees. They soon encountered the Wishing Steps, an ancient staircase leading down a steep portion of the trail.

"Oh! This is a special place," Lana called out. "If you want to make a wish come true, you have to walk down the stairs backwards and with your eyes closed, while thinking about it."

"Are you serious?" Nina asked, then looked to her husband and his father. All three grinned and rushed to the top step.

"First one down gets a double wish!" Nina called out.

"Step aside, children, elder coming through!" Patrick yelled, pushing the younger ones to the side with his umbrella.

Evelyn and Devon burst out laughing, but neither made a move to mimic their movements.

"Don't you want to make a wish?" Lana asked the Rileys.

"No need. I already got what I wanted." Evelyn smiled and kissed Devon's hand. "I got my husband back. Guy's death set Devon free."

That's an odd way of putting it, Lana thought, though her choice of words jogged a distant memory.

Before she could respond, the first O'Toole reached the bottom.

"I win!" Paddy yelled, pumping his fists in the air after he beat his wife and father by a significant margin.

"Besides, wishing doesn't make things happen," Evelyn said. "I've been wishing for Devon to find a way to restart his career ever since that article was published, but it never happened. Sometimes you have to take charge of your own destiny."

"Like when I told Guy off," Devon said proudly.

Evelyn's smile wavered. "Yeah, that's what I meant."

"And you, Lana? Are you going to wish for something?" Devon asked.

"That's a great idea! Actually, there is something…" Lana raced to the stairs and stepped down backwards, stumbling a little as she went. It was an unusual experience walking down an uneven flight of stairs with your eyes closed.

"What did you wish for?" Nina asked when she returned to the group.

"World peace," she joked, unwilling to share her real wish with them—to see Jeremy go free.

Yet, Lana knew that if she was going to make her wish come true, she was going to have to puzzle out which one of her guests had actually murdered Guy before the trip ended.

As they continued down the uneven path, Lana's mind raced through her list of suspects. Try as she might, Devon remained the strongest one. His laugh drew her attention up ahead. Evelyn was tickling him with leaves, and he was dancing around to get away. Devon was a changed man since confronting Guy, and his wife also seemed so much happier. It was now clear to Lana that Evelyn had been as adversely affected by Guy's article as Devon had been.

Evelyn's odd remark at the Wishing Steps niggled at her brain. A ray of sunlight bursting through the treetops lit up the path and triggered a memory in Lana's mind. After the group's first encounter with Guy, Devon had said that he would never be free, as long as the reporter was alive.

"Oh, no." Lana paled as she realized there was one guest she had never suspected. Could Guy's murder have been a crime of passion committed, in this case, by a wife hoping to help her husband recover his self-worth?

Jeanie wasn't the only drama queen on this trip, she grasped, recalling Evelyn crying about Devon's lost luggage, complaining about his disinterest in art, obsessing about their Celtic rings, and declaring adamantly that she didn't want to live with a corpse.

And what had Patrick said about family? That most would do anything to protect those they love, but that sometimes they went about it the wrong way.

Evelyn had said that Guy had extinguished Devon's passion for life. Had Evelyn done what she believed she had to do, in order to reignite it? *What a waste*, Lana thought. If only Evelyn had heard Devon standing up to Guy, she would have known that there was no need to harm him. But she hadn't heard them talking, which meant Evelyn must have killed Guy to protect Devon.

Oh, lordy—Evelyn killed Guy.

Distracted by her flash of insight, Lana promptly tripped over a tree root sticking up out of the path, falling hard to the ground.

She cursed the tree and her luck, just as Devon and Evelyn scurried back to help her.

"Are you alright, Lana?" Evelyn asked, concern etched in her face as she held out a hand.

Lana ignored it and rolled back onto her haunches, staring up at her client. "It was you, wasn't it? You killed Guy. That's how your wish came true."

Evelyn backed up and lost her footing, falling onto her backside.

Devon stared at Lana, then his wife, both hunkered on the ground. "Ev, what did she just say?"

"Nothing—it's not true!" she screamed as she scrambled to her feet.

Lana was faster. She knew there was no way she could restrain Evelyn, especially if Devon sprung to her aid, but she wanted to have a fighting chance at chasing after her, in case it was necessary.

Devon stood frozen to the ground. "What did you do, Ev?"

"I did it for us!" she cried.

"You murdered a human being for *us*? How could you say that? I wouldn't wish my worst enemy dead." He tore at his hair as tears rolled down his cheeks. "Now I'm going to lose my real lucky charm—you."

Evelyn glared at him. "Stop your whining. That's why I did it—to stop your tears of self-pity. Since that article came out, you've been a shell of your former self. It's as if Guy's words sucked the life and joy right out of you. I was tired of living with the pathetic, washed-up person you had become. I wanted my husband back!"

Devon stared at her. "You didn't do this for us; you did it for you."

"No, I—" She took a step forward and reached out to him, but Devon recoiled from her touch. Evelyn threw her head into her hands as sobs racked her body.

Her husband stood by, impassively watching her outburst. To Lana, he seemed more disgusted than distressed. "But I told Guy how I felt! I confronted him on my own, without using violence, Evelyn. I felt like my old self the moment I stepped away from him."

"I wish I had seen that happen, darling. I only wanted to protect you from him. When I couldn't find you on the dance floor, I went to our table but you weren't there. I figured you were still in the bathroom, which is where Guy seemed to be heading. I was so worried he would torment you again. When I stubbed my toe on that stupid leprechaun statue, I grabbed it, in case I needed to fend him off."

"Why did you have to kill him?"

She lowered her head, as if the truth was too painful to face. "Devon, when I entered the hallway, the alleyway door opened, then quickly closed again. In that instant, I saw you walking away from Guy as he lit up a cigarette. I figured he had belittled you and chased you away. Can you imagine how powerless that made me feel?"

Her husband looked at her through slitted eyes, as if he was seeing her for the first time.

"I raised the statue over my head and pushed the door open with my hip. Guy turned towards me when I did, so the statue caught his forehead. I wanted to hurt him, not kill him. But it was heavier than I realized, and it came down harder than I had expected. He fell over and then the blood…"

Evelyn sucked in a lungful of air, and her eyes fluttered shut. "I knew he was dead. I didn't know what to do, so I fled to the bathroom to wash my face. When I came out, a girl was screaming about someone being murdered and Jeremy had Guy's blood on his hands."

"Did you intentionally frame Jeremy by using that statue to hit Guy?" Lana dared to ask.

"No! If I hadn't stubbed my toe on it, I wouldn't have picked the statue up. I didn't mean to implicate Jeremy and feel horrible that he was arrested."

Not enough to tell the police the truth, Lana thought, a ball of anger swelling inside her.

Evelyn looked up at Devon sheepishly. "When we found each other again, after Guy had been killed, you kissed me so passionately, just like you used to. That made me feel like I had done the right thing."

The love in her eyes clearly tore at Devon's soul. Lana could almost see the poor man's heart breaking.

He wrapped his arms around his wife. "Oh, Ev. I love you more than you know. I'm so sorry—for everything."

Devon turned to Lana and asked softly, "What happens now?"

"We call the police." *And Jeremy goes free*, she added in her mind.

32

A Parade Fit for a Saint

March 17—Day Six of the Wanderlust Tour in Dublin, Ireland

"*Sláinte!*" Jeremy cried out, holding a green beer up high in the air. Kitty and Lana clinked glasses with him, giggling as they did. Ever since he had been released from police custody twelve hours ago, neither woman could get the grin off of their faces. The parade passing in front of them seemed to mirror their frivolity.

Their view of the Saint Patrick's Day parade from the VIP grandstands at Parnell Square was perfect, and the roof protected them from the many bursts of rain. Floats and bands were lined up as far as Lana's eye could see. From high school bands to meticulously crafted animatronic floats, the annual parade was a mishmash of all things Irish.

Clowns, DJs, dancers, acrobats, crazy bicyclists, and bagpipers were interspersed throughout the parade. Gigantic floats illustrating mythical beasts and Irish folklore—some towering several feet above the festival-goers—thrilled the crowd. Clydesdale horses pulled a golden carriage along the route, its occupants furiously waving at the massive crowd. The many children taking part in the parade were dressed in colorful bee, butterfly, and flower costumes. Lana loved the fairy costumes most of all; the little girls looked so cute with their glitter wings and vibrant face paint.

Randy was standing in front of them making short films of the parade for his wife while narrating them with silly stories about their week's adventures. Sitting behind them were Jeanie and the bartender from The Hairy Lemon who had bandaged her head wound. They were snuggling close as they watched the festivities cheek to cheek. *Jeanie had come to Dublin for love, and she found it*, Lana thought, chuckling at the path her client had taken to find it.

Paddy, Nina, and Mitch were dancing in the aisle to the beat of the many bands passing by. Even Patrick was getting into the spirit, though from a seated position and with a green Guinness in his hand.

Evelyn was now in police custody, and Devon was presumably arranging a lawyer for her. Lana wondered how many years in prison she faced, but one look at Jeremy made her forget about the Rileys.

She was so glad that Jeremy's parents had insisted they stay on three more days, so that he and Kitty could see more than just the police station before they flew home. Dotty took care of the plane tickets, and Lana paid for the hotel.

When a cluster of leprechauns danced by, the children's fake red beards adding a comic touch to the performance, Jeremy and Kitty tensed up.

"Are you going to buy a new leprechaun statue to replace the other one for your girls?" Lana teased.

"No!" responded Jeremy and Kitty simultaneously.

"We have enough other souvenirs to buy and places to visit. We can't thank you enough, Lana, for changing everything around so we can stay longer. Ireland is a magical place. It would have been a shame not to see more of it."

"So, this experience hasn't ruined your appetite for travel and adventure?" Lana asked.

"No, but next time we will stay closer to home. We could drive to the beach," Jeremy offered, as he looked to his wife. "There are plenty of beautiful places to visit on the Washington coast. We could rent a hotel room for us and the girls, and one for my parents."

"Great idea!" Kitty kissed her husband's cheek before turning to Lana. "What about you? Are you heading back to Seattle or do you have another tour to lead?"

"Alex and I are supposed to be meeting up in Amsterdam for a long weekend, before I lead a tour through Andalucía the first week of April. Our group will be in Seville for Easter."

"Oh, Spain is high up on my bucket list, as well," Kitty said dreamily.

"When the girls are old enough to travel with us," Jeremy replied, his tone resolute. "I'm not going anywhere again without them."

"I'll hold you to it." Kitty wagged her finger at him.

A high school band striking up drew their attention back to the parade. Drummers and dancers tippity-tapped their flags in time with the music as they passed by.

"What a fabulous way to celebrate Saint Patrick's Day!" Lana enthused.

The three raised their glasses in the air again. "To Dublin!"

"And great friends," Kitty adding, squeezing Lana's shoulder as she did.

THE END

Follow the further adventures of Lana Hansen in *Death by Flamenco: An Easter Murder in Seville.*

When a renowned travel writer is killed during a flamenco workshop, tour guide Lana Hansen is one of the Spanish police's prime suspects. Can she sleuth out the killer's true identity and dance her way out of a jail sentence before her group's tour to Seville is over?

Now available as paperback, Large Print edition, and eBook.

Thanks for reading *Death by Leprechaun*!

Reviews really do help readers decide whether they want to take a chance on a new author. If you enjoyed this story, please consider posting a review on BookBub, on Goodreads, or with your favorite retailer. I appreciate it!
Jennifer S. Alderson

Acknowledgments

I want to thank my wonderful family for helping me create the time and space to write during the many lockdowns and school closures.

My editor, Sadye Scott-Hainchek of The Fussy Librarian, continues to do an excellent job polishing this series, and I am grateful for her outstanding work and advice. The cover designer for this series, Elizabeth Mackey, constantly amazes me with her gorgeous and fun designs.

I hope this book and the others in my Travel Can Be Murder series help to sate your wanderlust during these trying times. Stay safe, dear readers. As the Irish say, *sláinte*—"to your health!"

About the Author

For more information about Jennifer's upcoming novels, please visit her website [www.jennifersalderson.com] or sign up for her newsletter [http://eepurl.com/cWmc29].

Jennifer S. Alderson was born in San Francisco, raised in Seattle, and currently lives in Amsterdam. After traveling extensively around Asia, Oceania, and Central America, she moved to Darwin, Australia, before finally settling in the Netherlands. Her background in journalism, multimedia development, and art history enriches her novels. When not writing, she can be found in a museum, biking around Amsterdam, or enjoying a coffee along the canal while planning her next research trip.

Jennifer's love of travel, art, and culture inspires her award-winning Zelda Richardson Mystery series, her Travel Can Be Murder Cozy Mysteries, and her standalone stories.

Book One of the Zelda Richardson Mystery series—*The Lover's Portrait*—is a suspenseful whodunit about Nazi-looted artwork that transports readers to WWII and present-day Amsterdam. Art, religion, and anthropology collide in *Rituals of the Dead* (Book Two), a thrilling artifact mystery set in Papua and the Netherlands. Her pulse-pounding adventure set in the Netherlands, Croatia, Italy, and Turkey—*Marked for Revenge* (Book Three)—is a story about stolen art, the mafia, and a father's vengeance. Book Four—*The Vermeer Deception*—is a WWII art mystery set in Germany and the Netherlands.

The Travel Can Be Murder Cozy Mysteries follow the adventures of tour guide and amateur sleuth Lana Hansen. Book One—*Death on the Danube*—takes Lana to Budapest for a New Year's trip. In *Death by Baguette* (Book Two), Lana escorts five couples on an unforgettable Valentine-

ABOUT THE AUTHOR

themed vacation to Paris. In Book Three—*Death by Windmill*—Lana's estranged mother joins her Mother's Day tour to the Netherlands. In Book Four—*Death by Bagpipes*—Lana accompanies a famous magician and his family to Edinburgh during the Fringe Festival. In Book Five—*Death by Fountain*—Lana has to sleuth out who really killed Randy Wright's ex-girlfriend—before his visit to Rome becomes permanent. In Book Six, *Death by Leprechaun*, Lana will need the luck of the Irish to clear her friend of a crime. Book Seven—*Death by Flamenco*—will be released in December 2021.

Jennifer is also the author of two thrilling adventure novels: *Down and Out in Kathmandu* and *Holiday Gone Wrong*. Her travelogue, *Notes of a Naive Traveler*, is a must-read for those interested in traveling to Nepal and Thailand. All three are available in the *Adventures in Backpacking* box set.

Death on the Danube: A New Year's Murder in Budapest

Book One of the Travel Can Be Murder Cozy Mystery series

Who knew a New Year's trip to Budapest could be so deadly? The tour must go on—even with a killer in their midst...

Recent divorcee Lana Hansen needs a break. Her luck has run sour for going on a decade, ever since she got fired from her favorite job as an investigative reporter. When her fresh start in Seattle doesn't work out as planned, Lana ends up unemployed and penniless on Christmas Eve.

Dotty Thompson, her landlord and the owner of Wanderlust Tours, is also in a tight spot after one of her tour guides ends up in the hospital, leaving her a guide short on Christmas Day.

When Dotty offers her a job leading the tour group through Budapest, Hungary, Lana jumps at the chance. It's the perfect way to ring in the new year and pay her rent!

What starts off as the adventure of a lifetime quickly turns into a nightmare when Carl, her fellow tour guide, is found floating in the Danube River. Was it murder or accidental death? Suspects abound when Lana discovers almost everyone on the tour had a bone to pick with Carl.

But Dotty insists the tour must go on, so Lana finds herself trapped with nine murder suspects. When another guest turns up dead, Lana has to figure out who the killer is before she too ends up floating in the Danube...

Available as paperback, large print edition, eBook, and in Kindle Unlimited.

Death on the Danube
Chapter One: A Trip to Budapest

December 26—Seattle, Washington

"You want me to go where, Dotty? And do what?" Lana Hansen had trouble keeping the incredulity out of her voice. She was thrilled, as always, by her landlord's unwavering support and encouragement. But now Lana was beginning to wonder whether Dotty Thompson was becoming mentally unhinged.

"To escort a tour group in Budapest, Hungary. It'll be easy enough for a woman of your many talents."

Lana snorted with laughter. *Ha! What talents?* she thought. Her resume was indeed long: disgraced investigative journalist, injured magician's assistant, former kayaking guide, and now part-time yoga instructor—emphasis on "part-time."

"You'll get to celebrate New Year's while earning a paycheck and enjoying a free trip abroad, to boot. You've been moaning for months about wanting a fresh start. Well, this is as fresh as it gets!" Dotty exclaimed, causing her Christmas-bell earrings to jangle. She was wrapped up in a rainbow-colored bathrobe, a hairnet covering the curlers she set every morning. They were standing inside her living room, Lana still wearing her woolen navy jacket and rain boots. Behind Dotty's ample frame, Lana could see the many decorations and streamers she'd helped to hang up for the Christmas bash last night. Lana was certain that if Dotty's dogs hadn't woken her up, her landlord would have slept the day away.

"Working as one of your tour guides wasn't exactly what I had in mind, Dotty."

"I wouldn't ask you if I had any other choice." Dotty's tone switched from flippant to pleading. "Yesterday one of the guides and two guests crashed into each other while skibobbing outside of Prague, and all are hospitalized. Thank goodness none are in critical condition. But the rest of the group is leaving for Budapest in the morning, and Carl can't do it on his own. He's just not client-friendly enough to pull it off. And I need those five-star reviews, Lana."

Dotty was not only a property manager, she was also the owner of several successful small businesses. Lana knew Wanderlust Tours was Dotty's favorite and that she would do anything to ensure its continued success. Lana also knew that the tour company was suffering from the increased competition from online booking sites and was having trouble building its audience and generating traffic to its social media accounts. But asking Lana to fill in as a guide seemed desperate, even for Dotty, and even if it was the day after Christmas. Lana shook her head slowly. "I don't know. I'm not qualified to—"

Dotty grabbed one of Lana's hands and squeezed. "Qualified, shmalified. I didn't have any tour guide credentials when I started this company fifteen years ago, and that hasn't made a bit of difference. You enjoy leading those kayaking tours, right? This is the same thing, but for a while longer."

The older lady glanced down at the plastic cards in her other hand, shaking her head. "Besides, you know I love you like a daughter, but I can't accept these gift cards in lieu of rent. If you do this for me, you don't have to pay me back for the past two months' rent. I am offering you the chance of a lifetime. What have you got to lose?"

Printed in Great Britain
by Amazon